JJ Beazley

The Gift Horse

Prologue

From the musings of the ancient philosophers to the scripts of twenty first century films, the single question behind all attempts to rationalise the meaning of life and existence can be couched in a simple, four-word phrase. It is both agonisingly trite and sublimely profound: *What's it all about?*

Why do things happen the way they do? Why do people behave as they do? Is the universe unfolding according to some plan, or has order risen out of chaos purely by accident? Is it true that all the world's a stage and all the men and women merely players? Are we simply making entrances and exits on cue?

Are the Fatalists right when they claim that everything is predetermined, so that there is no point in trying to influence anything since there is no such thing as free will? Are the Determinists right when they argue that everything is unwaveringly ordered by the logic of cause and effect; and that free will, whilst its existence cannot be denied, is governed by the same logic and is itself entirely predictable?

After two and a half thousand years the philosophers are still debating the matter. I think it likely that they always will; for it seems to me that the great, four word question is simply too deep for the human mind to fathom.

But let us suppose, for the purpose of making sense of the narrative that follows, that some controlling influence really is at work. What form does it take? Is it sentient or some natural, automatic working of cosmic machinery? Are Zeus and Aphrodite still sitting on Mount Olympus, watching us and ordering our destinies on some great

3

chess board that we call life? And if they, or something like them, are playing games with us, is something or some process even bigger and more mysterious playing games with them - or at least ensuring that they play the game to the right conclusion?

What follows does not presume to answer the big question. It is merely a simple story, simply told. It is one small angle on a picture whose complexity continues to defeat much greater minds than mine.

Chapter 1

Paddy was a bum, and I owe him no apology for saying so. The expression is little used these days, but I can't think of a better word to describe him succinctly.

"Dipsomaniac" would be correct, but Paddy was too much of a character to warrant the precise, professional language of the academic. "Alcoholic" he certainly was, but the word carries a pejorative connotation that would be unfair to a man of simple honour and rough-hewn decency. "Down and out" would be more appropriately colloquial, but not strictly accurate. Paddy was sometimes very down but I never saw him out, not even when he had his nose rearranged by a house brick thrown at him as he lay sleeping on a park bench one morning. "Bum" is the best of words to describe Paddy; and it has to be said that he was a very affable bum.

He spent a large part of his time, at least during the warmer months, sitting on the porch of the building in which I worked. It was an old Edwardian house that stood inside the leafy environs of the local municipal park. Having been the home of the head park keeper for the first sixty odd years of its life, it had subsequently been turned over to use as offices by a department of the local council. When their new premises had been built in the town centre it had become redundant and they had leased it to my employer. Our main office was also in the town centre, but it had become too cramped and we needed extra space to take the overflow. Accordingly, seven of us had been willingly despatched to work in the quiet little satellite that nestled comfortably between a bank of gnarled old trees and the sinuous footpath that snaked off towards the centre of the park.

Paddy was often alone, but sometimes he had a gaggle of other bums for company. He didn't seem to mind either way. As long as he'd got a packet of cigarettes, something to light them with and a supply of cheap cider to smooth the passage of the long and uneventful hours, he was content.

I'd heard that he could be aggressive. He went missing occasionally and his companions would tell me that he'd been locked up in the local police cells, waiting to be charged with assault before being released on bail. That didn't bother me in the slightest. I knew that people in Paddy's position usually came to be there as a result of events or circumstances over which they had little or no control, and of which the rest of us have little or no experience. They tend to feel that society has treated them badly. Having driven them out into the mud, it won't let them back in now that they have become soiled. Even those who are there because of their own actions or inadequacies need to blame some external, invisible culprit and many of them feel permanently angry. Their outward show of self control under non-stressful circumstances is but a thin veneer that cracks easily when tensions mount. Aggressive behaviour comes easily to them, particularly amongst themselves. Paddy was no exception.

He was never aggressive towards me though, quite the opposite in fact. Unlike most of the people he encountered outside his small circle of like-minded friends, I treated him with respect; and he responded to the fact by affording me a level of courtesy that bordered on deference at times.

His real name wasn't Paddy, either; it was Kevin. But such a prosaic name didn't suit him, and the only person who ever used it was his sometime ladyfriend - another member of the small group of habitual drinkers who used to wile away their time on the porch or the lawn in front of the building.

There was no pattern to their attendance. Sometimes they would be there *en masse*, sometimes in small groups of two or three, and sometimes Paddy would be there alone. He came nearly every day, except during those interludes when he was a guest of the local constabulary. He was on his own the day he asked to borrow some money. The look in his eye was deferential and the musical lilt of the Ulsterman in his voice was nothing if not persuasive.

"Sorry to ask you this, David," he said with an air of genuine apology, "but I wondered if you could see your way to lending us a couple of quid to get some supplies in. I'll pay you back Thursday when I get my money, so I will."

I gave it to him willingly. I knew that he became homeless occasionally when he got himself evicted from his room at the YMCA, and I knew that he was unemployed and addicted to cheap booze. But I also knew that he was no beggar. He had too much pride for that. He'd never asked me for money before and I had no fear that it would become a habit.

"You're a gentleman, so you are," he said. "I'll definitely pay you back Thursday."

He didn't turn up on Thursday. He disappeared for a week and I assumed him to be in trouble with the law again. But he never forgot that he owed me the money. When he reappeared he reminded me of his obligation.

"I haven't forgotten that two quid I owe you mate," he said cheerily - and continued to say habitually for the next six months.

Then he disappeared again and a friend of his told me that he had somehow managed to buy a one way ticket back to his native Belfast. He wanted to go home, apparently - for good. It did occur to me, though only briefly, that I would never see my two pounds again; but I was unconcerned. It was a trifling sum to me and I was glad that it had done him a favour. I was more sorry that we wouldn't be having our little chats any more. I had grown to quite like him, and had developed an odd respect for his rough and simple view of life.

And then, several weeks later, I arrived at the building one Monday morning and there was Paddy. He was sitting on the old wooden bench that stood inside the covered porch. It was mid September and the calm air, combined with the hazy, low sun, promised one of those warm, still days that often crop up between the fall of high summer and the onset of the autumn gales.

Paddy, however, seemed to be at odds with the spirit of optimism that permeated the quiet park. The building faced south and so, at that early hour, the sun was still only skimming the front of it. The porch was in almost full shadow and I thought it odd that he should be sitting in the shade instead of basking in the glory of the early autumn sunshine.

"Hello Paddy," I said as I approached. I was genuinely pleased to see him and smiled broadly as I walked up the path. "I thought you'd gone for good."

"So did I mate, so did I," he said ruefully. "But it wasn't to be."

"What happened?" I asked.

"Oh, just some fellas over there didn't want me around, you know. Bit of trouble from way back."

His manner was subdued and his voice carried a note of resignation. I knew that he had once served with the British Army, and had done a tour of duty in his native city during The Troubles. He had never been inclined to talk about it and I had deduced that it was a sensitive subject. I imagined that it was probably the cause of his present predicament and didn't press him for details.

"So you're back to stay then, are you?"

"Maybe, maybe not. Who knows?"

He carried the air of a man long since resigned to go uncomplaining to whatever landfall the winds of fate blew him. But then the light of something suddenly remembered dawned on him and he said

"Oh, I've brought you this." His mood lightened slightly as he reached into his coat pocket and took out something small. "This is to pay you back for that money you lent me." He handed me a small medallion about an inch or so in diameter. "It's what got me back here, and there's something important I need to tell you about it."

The most conspicuous thing about the artefact was its weight. Although it was the size of a ten pence piece, it was noticeably heavier and I judged it to be made of iron. The shape was slightly irregular, as though it had been fashioned by hand in some way and not pressed mechanically or cast in a modern mould. It was approximately circular, but not perfectly so; and it was heavily worn, thinner at some parts of its edge than others. It had two relief motifs, one on either side, that had also suffered considerable wear. Their outlines were, however, still clearly identifiable.

One side carried a pattern of four rectangular shapes with rounded edges, arranged at right angles to each other within a single, larger square. It reminded me of a four leaf clover and I thought it a likely interpretation as I knew it to be an old Irish symbol of good luck. The other side featured a badly executed Christian cross. The upright was vertical but the horizontal bar had a pronounced tilt down to the right. The rough shape and the heavy wear made the whole piece look very old, as though it had been passed from hand to hand and carried in countless pockets and pouches for many an age.

"Where did you get this?" I asked him, impressed by its apparent uniqueness.

"Ah now, there's a story to that," he said, with an air of gravity that suggested I should take him seriously.

"When I went home, I went to stay with my sister. Everything was fine for a while, but then somebody must have tipped off these local lads that I was back, you know? I knew I'd upset them once but thought it might have been water under the bridge by now. Seems it wasn't.

"There was a knock at the door one night and they told me I'd to be out of Ireland within a week - or else. Don't like to think what the 'or else' might have been, but it wouldn't have been very nice, that's for sure. Trouble was, I didn't have any money to buy a ferry ticket, so what was I supposed to do? My sister hadn't any money either, bless her. She's trying to bring up seven kids on benefit. The ferry ticket's a week's food to them. She said she'd go to the local loan shark, a bastard by the name of Gerry Cox. But I couldn't let her do that now, could I? He's the sort who'd have your legs broken for a debt of twenty quid. And he sometimes expects favours from the women, if you know what I mean.

"'So what are you going to do?' she asks me. 'Don't know' I says. 'I'll think of something.'

"The next day I was sitting on a bench in this kiddie's playground just along the road. Just sitting there you understand, minding my own business, trying to figure out some way of getting the money together, when this woman comes up and sits down beside me. Ordinary looking woman she was: small, about my age, dressed like any body else - nothing special about her.

"'Hello Kevin,' she says to me, 'I hear you're in need of a bit o' luck.' I looked at her; never seen her before in my life. I knew she wasn't from round there; she'd an accent from the south somewhere. 'Do I know you?' I says to her. 'Not directly,' she says. 'But you did my brother a favour some years ago. Helped him out of a jam.' 'Did I now?' I says. 'You did,' she says. 'And who might he be?' 'Oh, you wouldn't remember him.' she says. 'It was a long time ago.'

"And then she gives me this medal thing. 'That'll bring you the luck you need,' she says, dead serious like. 'But I have to warn you: when you've had your luck, you've to give it to somebody else within the week or it'll be reversed tenfold, and that's a fact.' They were the exact words: 'reversed tenfold.' Then she says 'good luck to you now,' and walked away. And I still don't know who she was, or who her brother was, or what I'd done to help him. Must be something to do with my army days, I suppose.

"Anyway, the next day my sister's looking through the paper and tells me there's a horse running at Chester called Kevin's Dilemma, and it's priced at 40-1. 40-1, eh? I thought the bugger must have had three legs or something. Anyway, couldn't resist it, could I? I'd a couple o' quid in my pocket, so I went to the local bookies and put one of them on this horse to win. It romped

11

home; couldn't believe it. I went and bought a ferry ticket straight away, before I spent it on the pop.

"That was five days ago, so now I've got to give that thing to somebody else. I was tempted to keep it, so I was – I could do with some regular luck. But I remembered what the woman said and thought 'never look a gift horse in the mouth, Paddy me boy'. So it's yours now mate. Hope it gets you what you need. But don't forget to pass it on when you've had your luck."

It was a good story but, of course, I didn't take it seriously. Inwardly I scoffed. "Typical Irish blarney" was my private reaction, but I didn't insult him by letting it show.

"Thanks Paddy," I said with as much enthusiasm as I could muster. "I reckon that's your debt paid off."

"Aye, well, I reckon so," he said. "But just make sure you get rid of it when it's done its job. Wouldn't want to see you having problems, mate."

I put the object in my pocket and went about my day's work. I remembered it later when I got home and took another look at it. I was certain about the four leaf clover on one side, but was surprised that the cross on the other should have been made crooked. It would hardly have been difficult to make the horizontal bar straight. The clover leaves were clearly well crafted, so why not the cross? Was it meant to be the standard Christian symbol, or something else?

I had a theory and went to my computer to test it. I typed "Runic symbols" into a search engine and selected the first option on offer. The page came up and there was my tilted cross. The page listed the Nordic Futhark and the tenth symbol read

The tenth, Neid, represents the essence of desire, whether wanting or needing.

So it seemed that the symbolism was of mixed provenance, Celtic on one side and Viking on the other. But the meanings were complimentary - need and desire accompanied by the bringer of luck. I knew that there was a strong Viking element in the history of Ireland and wondered how old the medallion was.

I became intrigued at the possibility that I might be in possession of an artefact of genuine antiquity, and wondered whether it might even have a high monetary value. I decided to take it to the museum and get their opinion. I was uncertain as to how much right I would have to sell it, but I could always discuss the matter with Paddy. I would obviously give the money to him and was sure that he would be very glad of the windfall.

I put the medallion on the desk by my computer, meaning to transfer it to my briefcase when I collected my things together later. The museum was only a short walk from my office in the park, and I intended to take it in and get their opinion the following lunchtime.

How fortunate that I forgot. How fortunate that my mind was elsewhere when I collected my briefcase, and that the little iron object sat unnoticed on the desk when I left the house to go to work the next morning.

I shut my front door on the stroke of eight as usual and set off to drive the four miles to the park that was situated on the edge of the city centre. I had only travelled about half a mile when I realised that I had forgotten the medallion. I decided I had time to go back for it and looked for a convenient place to turn around.

The road I was driving on was the main access to the suburban estate on which I lived. It was a

13

long and fairly straight road and had a 30 mph speed limit, but hardly anyone kept to the limit and I was no exception. I must have been travelling at about thirty five to forty when I decided to go back, and saw that I was approaching a side street. I lifted my foot from the accelerator and started to break gently.

At that moment a young child of around three or four ran out between two parked cars a short distance ahead of me. My right foot went down hard and my chest was forced against the seat belt as the car slithered noisily to a stop. The child stood looking at me just a few short yards from the front bumper.

I sat, shaking slightly, for a few seconds and then got out to make sure that he was all right. His mother, who had been standing nearby, got to him before I did. She was in a state of near panic, and was so concerned for his welfare that she ignored my interest in the matter. She carried him away without affording me anything more than an accusatory glance. That was of little consequence. I was swamped with a sense of relief that the worst tragedy imaginable had been averted.

Being responsible for someone's death has always been one of my greatest fears. I dreamt once that I had murdered somebody. It was a vivid and realistic dream, and I found the weight of remorse, coupled with the fear of detection, so oppressive that it took me days to shake off the effects. As I climbed back into the car, it struck me that the medallion had saved me from that most awful of burdens. I realised that, had it not been given to me, everything would have happened that morning just as it had done - with one exception. I would have been slightly nearer to the child and my right foot would have been on the accelerator pedal instead of the brake. It would have made all the difference. I tried not to think of the consequences, and the appalling effect it would have had on the rest of my life. The fact was immediately apparent that I had been the beneficiary of the most outstanding piece of good luck. I turned back to fetch the medallion and then carried on to work.

Paddy was sitting outside the office as usual when I arrived. I told him about the incident and a look of satisfaction spread over his face.

"Well, that's it mate," he said confidently. "You've got to give it away now."

I told him what I had discovered about the motifs and how I had considered taking it to the museum for identification and age assessment.

"And how long would all that take?" he asked.

"Don't know," I said. "I doubt they'd have a local expert. They'd probably have to send it to the British Museum or something. A few weeks probably."

"No time then, is there? You've got to be rid of it within a week."

"Well," I said, trying not to sound too dismissive, "that's only if you believe in that kind of thing. And it could be valuable, you know."

He looked at me in a way that he had never done before. It seemed to combine shock and disdain in equal measure. He turned away as though he were trying to gather his thoughts, and then looked back at me.

"So you think my bit of luck on the horses and your business with the car was just coincidence, do you? And both happening the day after we got that medal thing. And you think it might be valuable? I'm surprised at you David. Of course it's fuckin' valuable. That's obvious, so it is. But you don't sell things

15

like that. Things like that aren't for sale. Give it away, boy, within the week, or it's the Devil will be taking you. Have some respect for things you don't understand. D'you want to risk having your luck turned round on you? Tenfold she said. Imagine that – tenfold!"

I wasn't used to being told off by Paddy, or anyone else for that matter, and was startled by the ferocity of his riposte. It was untypically aggressive, but also articulate and logical. I stood and thought for a moment while he lit a cigarette and stared into the distance, shaking his head.

Eventually I decided he had a point. Perhaps genuine talismans do exist, and I had to admit that the medallion did have a certain "air" about it. It would, indeed, be churlish to see the value of such an object solely in monetary terms and I felt slightly ashamed that I had ever done so. My attitude seemed suddenly typical of our modern preoccupation with material wealth and I prided myself on being above that. I felt inclined to be cautious, too. Having my piece of luck reversed tenfold was a prospect that hardly bore thinking about. I decided to forget the visit to the museum and concentrate instead on considering who should be the next recipient.

"Mm, perhaps you're right," I muttered quietly, but Paddy ignored me. I left him staring into the distance, drawing on his cigarette, and went into the building.

Chapter 2

The day was busy as usual, but my thoughts kept drifting back to the same question. Who should be the next lucky owner of the medallion? I ran through the list of all the people I knew well and found the deliberation more difficult than I had imagined. From what I knew of my friends, family and colleagues, it seemed they all had some need or other, and I wanted to give it to the one with the greatest and most genuine. By early afternoon I had decided to give it to Nigel Smith.

Nigel was a colleague who worked in an adjoining office. We were not exactly the best of friends, but I knew him well enough and liked him. He had always seemed honest, affable and generous, and was always ready with a helping hand for those in need. He had the outward appearance of being settled and content with his lot. He and his wife seemed happily established in their marriage of ten years standing and he was, as far as I knew, financially comfortable.

He did have one small weakness, though. He had married young and never lost his eye for a pretty girl; but he seemed to keep his instincts under control. The security of his marriage was, it appeared, of greater importance to him.

But I had learned that he was troubled by one great sadness. He and his wife desperately wanted children, but had been unsuccessful in ten years of trying. Tests had shown that there was no medical reason for his wife's failure to conceive as both parties were fully endowed with the necessary capabilities. It just hadn't happened. I wondered whether the medallion might do the trick and felt that it was the most worthy of the options at my disposal.

I considered how I should approach him. On the surface, he was not the sort to admit to any belief in the power of talismans and I felt hesitant at the prospect of explaining it in a way that would sound credible. I considered taking a light hearted approach, but was concerned that he would fail to take the warning seriously. I decided to treat the matter with proper gravity and do my best to convince him that the object seemed to work.

I took it into him and told him Paddy's story and my own. I explained that we had both received strokes of good luck shortly after coming into possession of the medallion and in ways that were of paramount importance to us. If it didn't happen in his case, there would be nothing lost. If it did, that would amount to a compelling reason to accept its efficacy and take the warning seriously.

He looked surprised and slightly discomfited by the gift. It was clear that he wasn't quite sure how to react and he smiled uneasily as turned the object over and over in his hand. His enthusiasm seemed forced as he said

"I suppose that's a four leaf clover on that side?"

"Yes," I said, "I'm sure it is."

"Why's the cross crooked on the other?"

"It isn't a cross. It's a Viking symbol, a rune called Neid. It's the tenth in the runic alphabet and signifies desire. I looked it up on a website. The two symbols together indicate that you'll be lucky and get what you most wish for."

"Oh," he said, still looking uneasy. "That's nice. So why've you given it to me?"

"Got to give it to somebody," I said, deliberately avoiding the sensitive issue of children. "Why not?"

He still looked doubtful but evidently resigned himself to accepting the gift. No doubt he was concerned not to offend me. That would have been typical of his nature and I knew that I could rely on it.

"OK," he said. "Thanks."

I nodded and left it with him, glad that I had discharged my duty to whatever power controlled the function of the medallion. I was naturally impatient to know whether the talisman would work the desired magic, but realised that there was no hope of that for a few months at least. My realisation was based, of course, on my presumption that what Nigel most wanted was to have children. The following day, my assessment of his priorities was to be challenged.

I arrived at the office slightly earlier than usual and assumed that I would be the first one in. I was surprised to find the front door open and the alarm turned off, but there was no cleaner in evidence. It was her practice to start work an hour and a half before the office officially opened and wait for the first person to arrive before going home.

I checked downstairs and found her tools and materials stashed in their customary place in the cupboard at the end of the hall, but there was no sign of her or any member of staff. As I arrived at the bottom of the stairs to go up to my office, I heard a door open and footsteps cross the landing. I began the climb and saw the slight figure of Natalie, our clerical assistant, approaching the top of the stairs. She half turned her head down and towards me.

"Morning Dave," she said in a voice that was lacking its usual chirpiness, and then hurried on along the adjoining piece of landing that led to her own office.

To all outward appearances, Natalie was very much the typical young woman of new-millennium youth culture. Still, as far as I knew, in her late teens, she carried herself with the shallow but persuasive confidence common among her emancipated generation.

There was no doubting the advantages nature had given her. She was certainly very good looking, and the lure of her seductive hazel eyes coupled with the lustrous glory of her long, raven-dark hair would have been mesmerising in one inclined to be content with the simple value of such gifts. I had always thought it sad that she could have been quite beautiful, but chose to be merely pretty and cheaply alluring instead.

She was of medium height, slight of form and had that classic, suggestive style of walk in which the hips rock up and down alternately. It reminded me of those two-stroke Victorian beam engines, the sort that were used to pump water from deep mines in the old days. And she held one hand slightly away from her body with the palm turned downwards, as though it were waiting for some non-existent dog, or grateful male admirer perhaps, to sit up and lick it. I had seen models do the same thing on catwalks.

I had always thought her walk to be silly and affected since it had never looked natural, but I assumed that it brought the required response from passing male motorists and workers on building sites. And the style of her dress was carefully managed to be as revealing, or at least intriguing, as the conventions of contemporary fashion would permit. Seeking the approbation of men seemed to be Natalie's primary interest in life. She even treated me to what she undoubtedly saw as her feminine charms now and then. I always tried to be polite in return.

But she looked different that morning, more reserved and less inclined to flaunt her obvious physical attributes. I had the notion that she looked embarrassed.

By the time I reached the top of the stairs she had disappeared into her office and I turned to walk in the opposite direction towards mine. And then I noticed that Nigel's door was open and was in precisely the right place to explain where Natalie had been when I came in. I put my head around it to see Nigel working earnestly at his computer.

"You're early," I said.

"Oh, hello," he said, as though I had disturbed his concentration. It sounded false. "Yes, there was something I left unfinished when I went home last night. Needed to get it done for today."

He looked embarrassed too, or so it seemed to me. Perhaps I was being unfair, I thought. Perhaps I had already formed an unsubstantiated suspicion and was expecting him to look embarrassed. There was no real reason to be suspicious. It was perfectly normal for Natalie to visit everybody's office in the course of her work. But it was one of those situations in which the combination of circumstances and body language throw a little switch somewhere deep in the perceptive faculties, and the thought inevitably flickers into existence: "there's something about this that isn't normal."

I unlocked my own door which stood at a right angle to his and walked in to begin my own day's work. At lunchtime my unsubstantiated suspicion was transformed into a near certainty.

It was just turned one o'clock. I was about to unwrap my packed lunch when I heard the sound of several male voices outside. They were raised in a tone of lasciviousness, and interspersed with drunken laughter. I got up and walked over to my window. The explanation was predictable enough. Natalie had walked down the path and was on her way to the car park situated beyond a wide verge and a line of trees that fringed the roadway. She had obviously run the gauntlet of Paddy and several of his friends.

I smiled as I thought that even Natalie, incorrigible seeker of male attention though she was, would probably draw the line some way short of Paddy and his friends. But the swaggering of her hips, the tightness of her jeans, the low cut top and the bareness of her midriff were nothing if not eye catching. Her appearance, when combined with the disinhibiting effects of alcohol and warm sunshine on a group of men with nothing better to do, was hardly likely to produce a polite or indifferent reaction. What could she expect, I thought?

I was about to turn back again when I saw Nigel approaching the men from the direction of the front door. I wondered whether he was about to remonstrate with them, but he didn't. He walked between the group without a word and I thought that unusual. He always spoke to them as we all did, if only to exchange some brief, polite greeting. I watched as he walked in the direction of the car park and saw that Natalie was about to pass through the trees.

Most of the car park was hidden from view in the summer when the trees were in full leaf, but the few cars that I could see included Natalie's little red Citroen parked on the top side. I saw her turn left, disappear from view for a few seconds, and then re-emerge walking towards her car. She unlocked the door, climbed in and then sat there. She didn't drive off.

I turned my attention to Nigel who was walking, more slowly than usual I thought, towards the same gap in the trees. He turned his head nonchalantly from side to side, just far enough to get a view back to the office in his peripheral vision. After he passed through the trees he turned left and his stride quickened. A few seconds later I saw what, by now, had become inevitable. He approached Natalie's car and climbed in through the front passenger door. The car remained stationery for half a minute or so, and then drove off.

It was one of those situations again: the combination of circumstances and body language. There could have been a perfectly innocent explanation for Nigel going somewhere with Natalie during their lunch break. It was those slight nuances of untypical behaviour that pointed to the more dubious conclusion.

My first reaction was to think that it was none of my business; but then another thought struck me. I remembered that it was the day after I had given Nigel the talisman. I realised that if this was his good luck coming to fruition, it would mean two things.

Firstly, it would demonstrate that his instinct to receive the favours of a pretty girl were more important to him than the sanctity of his marriage vows. I found such a prospect disappointing, but of no real concern to me.

The second was of much greater consequence. It would mean that he would need to pass the talisman on within the week or risk the possibility of suffering whatever consequences might be in store. Rightly or wrongly, I felt a sense of personal responsibility over that one.

23

I pondered the question all through my lunch break and kept coming back to the same point: maybe I was jumping to an entirely wrong conclusion. But I thought it important to know whether I was right - for his sake, not mine. I looked at my watch when I heard footsteps coming up the stairs. It was three minutes past two. The footsteps continued beyond the top of the stairwell, obviously proceeding in the direction of Natalie's office. I looked out of the window and saw that her car was back in the same bay of the car park, and Nigel was coming back through the gap in the trees. It wasn't long before I heard him go into his own office. I took a deep breath, knocked on his door and walked in.

"Hi," he said.

He looked different somehow, slightly flushed I thought. There was an air of something contrived and artificial about his manner. He was more chirpy than usual, but his eyes betrayed the same suggestion of embarrassment that I felt I had seen earlier. In short, he looked guilty. I considered sitting down, but decided to remain standing. This was probably not going to be easy.

"I saw you going out with Natalie at lunchtime," I said.

The expression on his face changed and he looked defensive for a second, but he covered it with a show of seemingly studied indifference.

"So?"

I remained silent, trying to find the right words to broach a delicate subject diplomatically. He pre-empted my attempt and continued.

"We were both going in the same direction. She gave me a lift."

His reply led easily to the obvious question.

"So why did you go out and come back at different times?"

His pretended nonchalance dropped away and was replaced with annoyance bordering on anger.

"Because it happened to work out that way. Anyway, what the fucking hell's it got to do with you?"

The question was rhetorical and I was inclined to agree. But his sudden show of belligerence was entirely untypical of him and suggested that my question had touched a nerve. My doubts all but disappeared.

"Only this," I said, trying to remain calm and objective in the face of his rising hostility. "What you do in your private life is none of my business, but I gave you that talisman yesterday. If you've had your 'bit of luck' today, you'd be well advised to give it away within the next week. That's all."

His manner changed again to one of sneering disdain.

"Oh, fuck off Dave. You don't expect me to believe that crap, do you?"

"Well," I said, "that depends, doesn't it? Did you have your luck today or not? If you did, then one side of the story seems to be true Why not the other?"

"Because it's bullshit. You're as bad as Sarah. I told her your stupid story when I got home last night and she believed it. Thinks it's going to help us have kids or something. She had me put it in a draw for safe keeping. So I can't give it away now, can I? Can't tell her about my 'bit of luck' with Natalie, can I?"

His expression took on a look of irritated resignation as he realised that he had effectively admitted his indiscretion.

"Oh, for God's sake! So I got inside Natalie's knickers at lunchtime. So what? It's not an affair or anything, just a one night stand. You know her - she's got a bloke for every day of the week. She must have been one short of the seven this week. There's nothing to it, so just fuck off. You're right: it isn't any of your business."

He took hold of one of the files on his desk and opened it in a show of dismissal. I felt that there was little else I could say in the circumstances and turned to leave.

"And, as for your precious curse," he said as I was opening his door, "don't worry, I won't be losing any sleep over it."

As the door opened fully I saw Mrs Evans, our book-keeper, waiting a few feet away by the corner of the banister. She said nothing to me but walked towards Nigel's door as I turned right to go back into my own office. I heard her say a few words to him and then saw her come back out without the pile of papers she had been carrying.

The sight of her worried me. I was concerned that she might have overheard the conversation through the closed door. The pitch of Nigel's voice had risen in proportion to his annoyance, and it was very possible that she had. I thought it typically furtive of her that she had managed to approach unheard, and wondered how long she had been standing there.

I had always found Mrs Evans the most difficult person to get on with. She had a starchy, intolerant sort of manner and was the most intractable, dyed-in-the-wool moralist I had ever known. She was married to a Methodist lay preacher, and was a staunch follower of the faith herself.

It wasn't her faith that concerned me, however. It was her sheer bloody-minded refusal to accept that any sort of alternative, let alone contrary, view could be worth

26

considering. She insisted that every word of the Bible was to be taken literally and simply refused to respond if the odd contradiction here and there was pointed out.

I had often heard her rail against other faiths and their holy books, claiming that they were all the work of the Devil, and that those who chose to believe in them were at worst paragons of evil and at best deluded fools heading for the certainty of hellfire and damnation. And it seemed to be a comfort to her that the members of the local Asian population, who we occasionally saw passing our windows, were destined to be going somewhere far removed from her appointed place of eternal rest at the Day of Judgement. At least they wouldn't trouble her there.

What troubled me, however, was that she was acquainted with Nigel's wife, Sarah. And, of course, she had her phone number. Discretion was not one of Mrs Evans' more obvious characteristics. Spitefulness was. My fear turned out to be well founded.

The following morning I heard raised voices coming from downstairs. Mrs Evans occupied the room directly beneath mine and it had already occurred to me that her window gave pretty much the same view of the car park. Being a keen observer of everything that went on outside, it was entirely likely that she had seen the same apparent tryst between Nigel and Natalie as I had. She would have leapt to the same conclusion, even without the additional evidence that had been available to me, and with much more certainty. And she would undoubtedly have regarded the goings-on as her business. Everything that fell within her definition of impropriety, let alone immorality, was her business.

A few minutes later Nigel came storming into my office. It seemed that neither the meeting in the car park nor our conversation in his office had eluded Mrs Evans' well honed faculties.

"That bitch Evans has only gone and phoned Sarah to tell her that I'm having an affair with the office tart," he said through clenched teeth. "She saw us getting in the car, didn't she? But it was our little confab that confirmed it. I wish you'd kept your fucking nose out of my business, you bastard. Sarah's moved into the spare room and the atmosphere's like a fucking lead weight. God knows whether she'll ever come round. You realise, don't you, that this could be the end of ten years of happy marriage?"

My first inclination was to point out that nobody had forced him to 'get into Natalie's knickers,' but I decided against confrontation.

"I came to see you out of a sense of duty," I said calmly.

"That's what the bitch from hell said as well," he said as he turned to storm back out of my office.

"But *I* did it for your sake," I replied. "And I still think you should give that medallion away."

"Bollocks," was the last thing I heard before his office door slammed.

In the whole of the three years I'd known Nigel, I don't think I'd ever heard him use as many expletives as he had uttered during two short conversations in the last twenty four hours. Perhaps he wasn't quite the gentle, home loving man I had thought him to be. But then, he was facing a crisis; and how many of us can honestly say that we have never risked something precious to us in a moment of weakness?

I wondered whether to pursue the matter of the talisman with him. I doubted that he would listen at the moment and realised that it would be better to give him time to calm down. But how much time? There were only six days to go before the mirror might crack and the curse come upon him.

Or would it? Perhaps I was being fanciful. How could I know? I decided that one more day would make little difference and got on with my afternoon's work.

Nigel left early that day. I heard his door slam and the key turn in the lock shortly after 4.30. The weather had turned wet and I watched him walk across to the car park, holding his raincoat closed with one hand and using his briefcase as a makeshift umbrella with the other. I thought he looked a lonely figure as he made his way across the sodden grass between the path and the trees. I felt a stirring of pity as I wondered whether he was heading for what was undoubtedly an oppressive atmosphere at home, or whether he was about to augment his new-found alienation with a couple of hours spent in one of the town centre bars. And I truly wished that I hadn't given him the talisman.

I packed my own things away at five o'clock as usual and checked the upstairs rooms. They were all locked. Each of the employees had a key to the outside door and it was the job of the last one out to set the alarm and lock up.

As I made my way downstairs, Mrs Evans was locking her own door. She ignored me and hurried out. Perhaps she thought she would be in for an argument if she spoke to me. I assumed that she had heard enough of the conversation to be aware of the talisman and I wondered what her attitude to it would be. No doubt she would consider it to be an artefact of the Devil himself, and that its very existence afforded all the vindication she needed for her actions.

The rest of the downstairs was empty and so I set the alarm, went out and locked the door. Paddy was standing alone inside the porch with his customary bottle and cigarette, obviously sheltering from the rain.

"Heard you having some shenanigans in that place of yours, the last couple of days," he said.

I saw no reason not to tell him the story. After all, he was directly involved.

"Can't understand some people," he declared, shaking his head. "Nice wife, home, all the things I'd give my right arm for, and he can't resist throwing it all away for the sake of one bit of humping with the wee minx. Can't say I've got much sympathy for him, have you?"

I decided not to enter into a discussion on the subject of human frailties and "moments of weakness." Paddy's views on life tended to be simple; they didn't really allow for shades of grey. I did observe, however, that Nigel might not have actually thrown anything away. Moments of infidelity were not that uncommon, I said, and reconciliation was entirely possible.

"Not if he doesn't get rid of that medal thing, it isn't," he replied with an air of certainty. "I'm damn sure of that."

Though still not entirely convinced, I thought he might be right and drove home with something of a weight on my mind. I kept reminding myself that I had given Nigel fair warning of the possible consequences and that there was no reason for me to feel guilty if he ignored it. I further reminded myself that the whole thing might be nothing more than a piece of prime Irish blarney anyway. And yet something still nagged and tugged at me inside. My sense of responsibility was outweighing my pleas to reason, and the need to persuade him to pass the medallion on was getting stronger.

Chapter 3

The problem was postponed by default the next day when Nigel failed to come into the office. I was neither surprised nor unduly concerned. It was Friday and I assumed that the need to sort out his domestic difficulties was taking precedence over the routine matter of employment. It seemed sensible enough to take a long weekend to pour oil on the troubled waters of his marriage.

It did occur to me, however, that I had only until the following Wednesday to persuade him to get rid of the talisman, but there was little I could do. Despite having worked with him for three years, I had never been to his house and had never had any reason to be given his phone number. I looked in the phone directory to see if he was listed. He wasn't. I knew that Mrs Evans would have it, but decided to forego the dubious pleasure of that option until it became absolutely necessary.

Mrs Evans was presenting a particularly frosty front to everybody that day, even by her standards, and Natalie was also keeping herself largely to her office. When she did make the odd, inescapable foray in the course of her duties, she was noticeably quieter and less ebullient than usual.

It struck me as ironic that their respective attitudes of reticence were both probably driven by feelings of guilt. In Mrs Evans' case, though, I had no doubt that her difficulty was more than adequately countered by the certainty of moral indignation. Natalie, I was sure, felt nothing more than a sense of circumstantial embarrassment. I thought it unlikely that the effect would spill over into her personal life as I doubted that her conscience was substantial enough to be seriously pricked.

Between them, however, they did manage to cast something of a shadow over the office and I was glad to go home that night. I hoped that Nigel would be back at work on Monday and felt that the weekend would give me the opportunity of working out a way to broach the thorny subject of the talisman again.

I was unsuccessful. The more I thought about it, the more bereft I felt of any cunning artifice that would achieve the desired breakthrough. There was nothing for it but another straightforward plea to reason. "If it's worked three times on the trot, it's worth taking the warning seriously" was all I kept hearing myself say. I went to work on Monday morning expecting another difficult day.

Nigel was absent again and there were the inevitable mutterings among the staff. His indiscretion with Natalie had become common knowledge by then, probably through the agency of one of Mrs Evans' moralistic diatribes. She was back to her strutting, sanctimonious best. Natalie, on the other hand, was clearly more discomfited than ever. She was in the building but was so withdrawn, both physically and mentally, that she might as well have been absent too.

He didn't turn up on Tuesday morning either. I rang the personnel department in our main office to enquire whether they'd heard anything. He'd sent in a sick note, they told me; he wouldn't be back for a couple of weeks. I asked what the problem was and they said that such information was confidential. Enough hints were dropped, however, to give me the predictable answer. "Nervous exhaustion," that old euphemism for depression. I asked if I could have his phone number but was refused. The rules forbade the giving out of employees private details, even to colleagues. It seemed that I would have to approach Mrs Evans after all.

I went downstairs to her office feeling some degree of trepidation. She was technically junior to me, but was possessed of that combination of intransigence and intolerance that I have occasionally observed in women of a certain age. It allowed no consideration of logic, rank or anything else to override the mood of the moment; and, when that mood was motivated by issues of morality, she was formidable. I knocked politely and went in.

"Have you got Nigel's phone number?" I asked with some attempt at nonchalance.

"Why?"

Her mouth was turned sharply down at both corners and her eyes carried a look that said "this is a challenge and I don't intend to lose."

"Because I want to phone him, why else?" I felt an immediate sense of irritation but struggled to subdue it.

"There's no obligation on me to give it to you. In fact, it would be in breach of the data protection laws."

This was pretty much what I'd expected.

"If you were in personnel I would agree," I said calmly. "But this is a local matter. Nigel's a friend. He's ill and it's perfectly reasonable to want to see how he is - offer support, that kind of thing."

"Have you looked in the phone book?"

"Yes. He's ex-directory."

"Doesn't want to be contacted then, does he? It's not my business to give you his phone number."

She turned back to the keyboard and started typing numbers into a spreadsheet. I couldn't help stating the obvious.

"You considered it your business to tell Nigel's wife about Natalie."

"That was quite different," she said confidently, without taking her eyes from the screen. "Numbers, Chapter 32: 'Be sure your sin will find you out.'"

I felt annoyed again. I knew already that Mrs Evans was one of those people who believe that being able to quote chapter and verse of the Bible somehow gives them the monopoly on rightness. I also knew that the Bible could be quoted to justify almost anything, and had long considered such an attitude to be one of the worst forms of religious bigotry. I couldn't match her facility, of course. I could only proceed with general principles.

"Oh come on, surely it's a good Christian virtue to want to help someone in trouble."

She turned back to face me. Her eyes carried a look of thinly disguised mockery this time.

"Are you a good Christian then?"

"No, I'm not," I said, feeling the irritation rise again. "But you are, aren't you?"

The frost reasserted its grip on Mrs Evans' features. No doubt she had detected the inevitable note of sarcasm in my voice and her reply carried a clear tone of smug self-satisfaction

"I think good Christian virtues would be wasted on our master Nigel."

She turned away again. She would have made a good Victorian schoolma'm, I thought. But I pressed on.

"But didn't Jesus say that the sinner was the one most in need of attention?"

"To bring him to a state of redemption, yes. But not to get him out of a filthy hole that he's got himself into."

She started typing again, clearly signalling that she regarded the matter as closed. I didn't.

"So what about the adulterous woman who was about to be stoned?" I continued. "Didn't Jesus order the crowd to forgive her? 'Let him who is without sin cast the first stone,' and all that."

Her hands came off the keyboard, her shoulders sagged and she sighed. She sat and stared into space for a few seconds and I could see the muscle in her jaw tightening and relaxing in rapid succession. I suppose she was trying to reconcile the conflict between her own defensive, unforgiving nature and the clearly stated command of her Lord and Saviour to forgive the sinner, even when the transgression involved adultery. It seemed I had found a chink in her armour - or maybe she just wasn't in the mood for arguing that day. She reached suddenly into her top drawer, took out an indexed book and thumbed her way to the right place.

"892764" she said without looking at me, then slammed the book shut, threw it back into the drawer and resumed her typing.

"Thank you," I said and left.

All in all, it had been easier than I had expected. Her defences must have been at a low ebb for once. I returned to my office, very pleased with myself, and scribbled the number on a sheet of scrap paper. And then I picked up the phone and dialled it. A female voice answered.

"Is that Sarah?" I asked.

"Yes."

"Oh, hello, it's David from the office. Could I speak to Nigel please?"

"No," she said and hung up.

I stood in a mild state of shock for a few seconds, holding the phone while I overcame my sense of disbelief. All that effort dismissed in a single word of one syllable. I replaced the receiver and decided that I owed it to my own sense of pride and duty to persevere. I called the number again and the same voice answered.

"What?" she said in a tone of annoyance. She probably guessed that it was me.

"It's David again. Look, I really do need to speak to Nigel."

"Well you can't. He's not here."

"Can you tell me when..."

There was no point in continuing. She'd hung up again. Whether she was telling the truth, or whether she was just determined to monitor all incoming calls I had no way of knowing. I decided that she probably blamed me for Nigel's infidelity. I decided to try again later that evening. There was only one day to go.

I rang at eight o'clock but there was no reply until a voicemail message cut in. I had a mental image of Sarah standing between Nigel and the phone, daring him to risk dire retribution if he so much as moved. I left a message anyway, just in case he found the chance to pick it up. I wasn't hopeful. If my image of the happy scene was anywhere near accurate, I assumed that Sarah would delete it immediately. I knew he had a mobile, but hadn't a clue what the number was. And I assumed that even the well organised Mrs Evans wouldn't have it either; she saw herself as a friend of Sarah's, not Nigel's. I doubted that anyone in the office would have it, since our work was not the sort that required the contacting of people outside office hours.

Except, perhaps, Natalie - he might have given it to her. Why hadn't I thought of that before? Wednesday would be my last chance to save Nigel from whatever dire consequences were waiting to befall him. I could think of no other course than to hope that Natalie might prove to be his salvation.

She wasn't. I went into her office first thing and asked the question. She blushed when I mentioned Nigel's name and shook her head.

"Sorry," she said quietly in a pathetic, helpless sort of way. I felt almost sorry for her.

My real concern, of course, was for Nigel. All I could do now was to hope that there was nothing to the curse story after all. I thought back to the events of the previous week, starting with Paddy's original story. I wondered just what the odds were against three people having strokes of good fortune in ways that were of major significance to them, all on the day following the receipt of a supposed good luck charm. There was no way of calculating such odds, but something about the story suddenly struck me as odd. I mulled it over for a few minutes and then went outside to see if Paddy was in attendance that day. He was sitting alone on the low wall that bordered the path. We exchanged a few brief pleasantries and I sat on the wall opposite.

"There's something a bit odd about this medallion business," I said.

"Oh aye? What's that?"

"Well, the story goes like this, right? The talisman brings you good luck and then you've got to pass it on to somebody else within a week or something dreadful will happen."

"Right."

"Well, you and I both had our luck the day after we got it and we passed it on in good time. Nigel also had his luck the next day and I don't know whether he's passed it on yet, but that's not the point. The point is this: anybody who believes in the talisman isn't going to give it away until he or she has had their luck, and then they know they've got a pretty tight time limit to get rid of it. And if they don't believe in it, they're not likely to be giving it to somebody in all seriousness and making up some cock-and-bull story about a curse, are they?"

"Suppose not."

"So what about the woman who gave it to you? Isn't it a bit difficult to believe that she was given the thing, had her luck and then just happened to hear about your problem within the week? Somebody you don't know? Somebody who tells you some mysterious story about an old debt involving her brother? Something you don't even remember? I mean, who is she? Why suddenly appear out of the blue like that? I suppose it's possible, but it's all a bit of a coincidence isn't it?"

Paddy raised his eyebrows, thought for a while and then shrugged his shoulders.

"Don't know, mate. Who do you think she was?" he asked eventually.

"I haven't a clue. I wasn't there, was I? Can you remember anything else about her, apart from what you told me? How old was she? What did she look like? What colour hair did she have?"

It occurred to me as I was asking the questions that they would be unlikely to help solve the mystery. I was just clutching at straws. And Paddy shook his head anyway.

"There's no point in asking me things like that, David. I remember her giving the thing to me and pretty much what she said, 'cos that was all a bit strange, you know? But I wouldn't remember details. You must have noticed the effect the drink has on people like us. We can't even remember what we did this morning sometimes, let alone two fuckin' weeks ago."

I had noticed it. One of the difficulties of talking to Paddy and his friends was having to sit politely through the same recollections and recriminations that I had heard several times before. And often the previous telling had only been a few hours before the present one.

"Oh well, I suppose it'll just have to remain a mystery," I said, rising to my feet. "Perhaps it was all light hearted and our bits of good luck were just coincidence. There probably is no curse."

"I wouldn't be so sure about that," he replied with a shake of his head. "I can tell you this David. That woman was deadly fuckin' serious, so she was. That much I *do* remember."

I walked back into the office feeling uneasy. My rational faculty wanted to treat the whole thing as a silly superstition. But one bit of that same faculty kept on reminding me that three people having a notable slice of luck, albeit dubious in Nigel's case, was stretching the probability of coincidence a little too far. And poor old Nigel was having his fair share of difficulty already, even before the appointed deadline. How much worse might things be likely to get from tomorrow onwards? I felt some sense of guilt at the prospect of merely leaving him to his fate, but what else could I do?

Chapter Four

Another week went by without any sign of Nigel's return to work. His sick note was due to expire the following Thursday and we had a call from personnel to tell us that it had been renewed for another two weeks. The job of reviewing his workload and dealing with anything that couldn't wait that long fell to me. It was that task that caused me to be late leaving the office on Friday evening.

It was around 6.30 when I locked up. I remember thinking that it was the first time in a good many months that I had needed to turn the hall light off before closing the door. An early October gale had been buffeting the windows all afternoon, and the daylight had risen and fallen as great masses of dark storm clouds swept across the sky. For the previous hour the cloud cover had been unremittingly heavy and the dusk had fallen early.

I walked unsteadily across the path and the grass verge that led to the car park. Occasionally I was forced to lean sideways into the teeth of the vicious, gusting gale. The line of trees that lay ahead of me were swaying frantically and the cacophony of hisses and whistles rose at times to an almost deafening crescendo. Small bits of broken branches were falling around me as I walked, and the air was filled with a blizzard of dry and shrivelled leaves. As I passed between the trees I saw that there were only two vehicles remaining in the park. One was mine and the other, standing in the next bay, I recognised as Nigel's. The driver's door opened as I approached. He got out and stood waiting for me.

Despite the growing gloom, I could see him well enough and knew immediately that he was considerably out of sorts. There was none of the usual bright and confident air about him. He looked thinner, especially about his face which was pale and stubbled for lack of shaving. His shoulders drooped as he stood with his hands in his pockets and he kept looking away from me as I stared steadfastly at him.

As I came close he turned his eyes briefly towards mine whilst keeping his head at a slight angle. I knew instinctively that this was the body language of a man with something troubling him, something that he probably wanted to talk about but which he evidently knew was not going to be easy.

"God, Nigel, you look rough," was my sadly predictable opening.

He dropped his head and nodded slightly.

"I need to talk to you," he said, a little weakly and with an air of apology.

"Let's get in the car," I said. "Get out of this wind."

We climbed in and shut the doors. The relative calm and quiet were a relief, even though the car shook sometimes from the force of a particularly strong gust, and bits of arboreal debris occasionally clattered against the windscreen.

"Do you mind if I smoke?" he asked in a way that sounded more like a statement of intent than a genuine question.

I shook my head but opened one of the back windows slightly to draw the smoke out of the car. He lit a cigarette with shaking hands and drew on it deeply. I waited for him to begin. He was obviously in no mood for pointless pleasantries and came straight to the point.

"I'm beginning to wonder about that curse business," he began.

"You've still got the talisman then?"

"Yes. Don't know where it is, though. Sarah moved it – put it somewhere safe I suppose."

"So what's happened?"

He looked at me with a troubled and confused expression, then turned away to look out of the window. He took another long drag of his cigarette and looked down into the foot well. His voice was low and despondent as he related the events of the previous two weeks.

"The day Sarah got that phone call from Evans she reacted as you'd expect. Lots of crying, shouting, telling me what a bastard I was – that sort of thing. She moved her stuff into the spare room the same night. She's been sleeping in there ever since.

"There wasn't much I could do except stand there and take it. I apologised, promised it wouldn't happen again, told her I still loved her and all that stuff. I felt like shit. I really do love her, you know. That's why I went to the docs the next day to get a sick note. Couldn't face this place for a while, not with Evans and Natalie in attendance.

"Anyway, for the next week the atmosphere was bloody rough. She refused to speak to me or do anything for me – I had to cook my own meals, wash my own clothes, make my own bed. Not that the practical things bothered me much. I wasn't really interested in eating anyway and the rest of it was just a matter of doing bits and pieces as necessary. It was the tension that got me down. I blamed you sometimes for giving me that medallion, but I shrugged it off. I still didn't really believe in the damn thing. I just hoped that time would take care of things and Sarah would come around eventually. And then the nightmares started."

I thought I saw him shudder slightly as he drew on his cigarette again. He continued.

"It was last Wednesday night. I remembered during the day that I was supposed to get rid of the medallion within a week, and that the time was up. It didn't worry me. I still thought of it as superstitious nonsense. But maybe that was why the dreams started that night; maybe it was just a psychological thing. But they're so realistic and so sickening. And they're driving me round the bend, big time."

He paused again and seemed reluctant to continue. He flicked the ash from his cigarette into the ashtray and drew long and hard on it.

"So what were these dreams about?" I asked.

He took a deep breath and then exhaled forcefully.

"I woke up some time in the early hours – it was still dark - and thought I could hear noises coming from Sarah's room. I went out onto the landing and saw a light under her door. The noises were definitely coming from there and sounded like grunts and panting. I thought she might be ill or distressed for some reason, so I knocked. There was no reply. I opened the door and looked round it.

"There she lay on her back, legs spread wide, with some great hairy bloke on top of her pumping away like a mad animal. I felt sick and shocked – and jealous as hell. My first thought was to grab something and beat his fucking brains out. But then my head started to swim and my vision became hazy. It got darker and darker and I could see flashing pinpoints of light. Then everything went completely black and I woke up again in my own bed. It was still dark outside but my bedside lamp was on. That put the wind up me. I was sure it was off when I went to sleep.

"I sat up in bed and listened. The noises had stopped. I got up in a bit of a panic and went and

44

opened Sarah's door. Needless to say, she was on her own and sleeping peacefully. As I said, I put it down to some horrible nightmare brought on by the circumstances and tried to forget about it.

"But then the next night, the same thing happened again. I dreamt that I woke up again and remembered the previous dream. It was really weird. I knew that the last time this had happened, it had been a dream. But this time it didn't feel like a dream. But then it hadn't felt like a dream the first time – while it was happening, that is. So what was this? Another dream, or was it real?

"I felt confused, frightened, feverish. I could hear the noises again and sat there for a bit, trembling and sweating – one of those horrible cold sweats you get when you're ill. I didn't want to go and open the door but I couldn't stop myself; it was like I was being forced to go and watch.

"It was a bit different that time. He looked round at me as he was doing it. His face was weatherbeaten and leathery with lots of lines, and he was ugly as sin. He grinned at me with this horrible, triumphant sort of leer. He was a big ox of a man with long, wiry red hair. And then it was the same as before: I felt weak and giddy, and then woke up in my own bed. Everything was back to normal.

"The third night I was a bit wary of going to bed and, sure enough, it happened again. Everything was the same as before, only this time they both looked at me – and Sarah smiled while she grimaced and groaned with pleasure. And it's happened every night since, even though I go to bed late and it takes me ages to get to sleep. And every night they're in a different position – everything you could think of. But always they laugh at me, triumphantly – like they're really enjoying what it's doing to me. Like that's the real point of it all – to make me suffer. Nine nights on the trot now and I'm getting less and less sleep. I don't know how much longer I can put up with it."

"Probably one more night," was my instinctive response. "Reversed tenfold was what the woman said to Paddy."

"I know," said Nigel. "That's what I've been telling myself for the past few days. But what then? A dream's just a dream, isn't it? It's not the same as reality. If it's just a dream, I'm not really being paid back tenfold, am I? Or am I? It's certainly getting to me well enough. I keep thinking that I'm creating these dreams myself – and that there'll be ten of them – to make myself suffer and pay off my guilt for what I did. I keep hoping that that's all there is to it. But I can't really say I believe that, not now."

"Why now?"

There was another pause as he stubbed out his cigarette in the ashtray and immediately lit another. He gathered himself again.

"I've seen a change in Sarah, a weird change. All the belligerence has gone and she's started to cook my meals again and do the other jobs she used to do. 'Great' you might think; she's coming round. But she's not, I'm sure of that. She still refuses to speak to me except when it's absolutely necessary. But she's very calm about everything – content even. It's not natural. She seems perfectly happy and yet, apart from sticking a plate of something under my nose twice a day, it's as though I'm not there.

"I've tried to talk to her, but it's like trying to grab a handful of steam. She just evades every attempt at conversation, either by ignoring me altogether or giving way with a sort of patronising detachment. 'Yes Nigel,' 'No Nigel,' 'Of course Nigel,' – like she's talking to a child or an imbecile or something. I can't tie her down to anything and it's driving me nuts.

"Then I see her smiling quietly to herself, as though all's right with the world and she's got what she wants. But what's that? Revenge? I don't know. I've asked her if she wants a trial separation or something, but what does she do? She walks away with that sickly smile on her face. 'Of course not dear,' she says with that – that – oh, I don't know; that fucking stupid, stupid voice she's started using.

"I haven't known what to make of it, until this morning. I saw her through the open kitchen door, smiling and looking down at her stomach. Then she patted it gently and it hit me like a hammer, straight between the eyes. I suddenly realised why she was so content. She's pregnant, I'm sure of it. Call me fanciful if you want. Tell me there's no evidence. I've been telling myself that all day. But I can't believe it. I just know there's something growing inside. And I know it's not mine. That's why I had to come and see you."

He looked me full in the face and the sudden transfer of some responsibility onto my shoulders took me by surprise. I hesitated and then asked the obvious.

"What can I do?"

"You seem to know about these things," he continued. "If this thing really is some kind of curse and the dreams really happened in some way, I couldn't live with bringing up that creature's brat. I need to know if it can be reversed."

It was my turn to look away as he stared at me. Much as I wanted to help, I was at a complete loss to know what to say that would be constructive. I looked back at him and shook my head.

"Honestly Nigel, I don't know anything about these things. I suppose I keep an open mind. I suppose I even believe in them up to a point. But I don't know anything about talismans and curses - how you put them on, how you take them off, anything like that."

"But you're the only person I know who might have some idea where to look," he said.

The expression in his eyes carried more than mere hope; there was note of pleading in them, a slight but unmistakeable sign of desperation. I thought for a few seconds and my brain cleared.

"Hang on," I said. "Firstly, you don't know that she's pregnant, do you? It seems likely to me that Sarah might *think* she is because she wants to believe it. It could be her way of dealing with the trauma of your having a fling with Natalie."

He shook his head and smiled ruefully.

"You don't know Sarah. I do; I've been married to her for ten years. She's hard as nails when the chips are down. She doesn't do imagination. That's not her way, believe me."

His voice carried such an air of certainty that arguing with him seemed pointless.

"OK," I continued, "second possibility. Suppose she is pregnant. How do you know it's not yours? You've been trying long enough, haven't you?"

"Exactly," he replied in the same dismissive tone. "Too big a coincidence, isn't it? Ten years of trying and it happens now? No, don't believe it. Besides, it doesn't make sense. She's hardly been through the door since all this blew up and, even then, it's only been to go to the supermarket and back. How would she have found out she was pregnant? I suppose she could have got one of those kits from the chemist, but she just wouldn't have behaved like that. It just isn't her."

My theories still seemed entirely plausible to me. I was inclined to think that Nigel's reaction was illogical and brought on by the stress he was under. But a small doubt remained even in my mind. I couldn't deny the fact that I had come to believe in the curse myself, and something like this did seem to fit the bill, however ludicrous it might appear. Maybe the dreams did constitute some form of reality. Maybe the ugly, wild haired ox of a man really was some sort of an incubus, given grotesque genesis by whatever mysterious force lay behind the talisman. I had never been one to instantly dismiss a strange possibility just because it was strange.

Whatever the truth of the matter, it was clear that Nigel needed a solution, either to lift the "curse" if it really existed, or at least to put his fevered imagination to rest.

"OK," I said, "I'll have to give this some thought. Perhaps I can get some information or find someone to talk to. I'll make it my project over the weekend and see what I can come up with. I'll do my best."

He nodded and tugged the door handle.

"Another night to go yet. God, I hope this is the last."

He pushed the door open and started to get out.

"Oh, nearly forgot." He stopped and handed me a piece of paper. "That's my mobile number. Call me on that when you come up with something, would you? I'd prefer to talk about this out of Sarah's hearing. Thanks."

He got out, slammed the door shut and walked the few feet to his own vehicle. I saw him get in, light yet another cigarette and drive away without so much as a wave.

I sat for a while pondering the situation. It seemed unlikely that the local library would have any serious tome on the mechanism of lifting curses and I couldn't think of anyone I knew who might be knowledgeable on the subject either. I briefly considered making something up, just to put Nigel's mind at rest; but that would have been dishonest, especially as my still, small voice kept reminding me that the curse might be real. I drove home without any ideas other than trying the library. I decided to go the following morning.

I spent three hours there examining every book I could find that might have carried some hint of a solution. It came as no surprise to find that all references to talismans were either superficial or academic. There was nothing of a practical nature. I spent further time in the afternoon rummaging through the mighty sludge of the internet, but ran out of patience at the umpteenth unhelpful website. I racked my brain in an attempt to think of someone I knew who might have some knowledge on the subject. I even rang a couple of people I hadn't spoken to for years. Neither of them could help and I went to the office on Monday morning wondering how Nigel would react when I told him there was nothing I could do. As I was settling into my daily routine, Natalie knocked on my door and walked in.

I hadn't seen much of her during the previous couple of weeks. She had continued to keep herself largely to her office, only venturing forth when absolutely necessary and, even then, confining herself to the briefest of questions or explanations before disappearing again.

But, on that Monday morning, she stood by my desk holding a piece of paper, apparently awaiting my attention. I glanced up at her and suddenly noticed how different she looked. Her style of dress, although still young and contemporary, was less provocative than usual. The jeans were as tight as ever, but she was wearing a long, loose-fitting sweater that came half way down her thighs. And the neckline was so high that it covered the lower part

50

of her throat. Even her hair was pulled back and held with a simple black band. More than that, she had a profoundly different air about her, or so it seemed to me. It was more sober, less flighty. But the most striking physical difference lay in her eyes. They were blue. I made the obvious comment with my usual directness.

"You've got blue eyes. I could have sworn they were brown."

"Coloured contacts," she said.

I had heard of such things but had no direct experience of them. I completed the conversation, purely for the sake of politeness, with a perfunctory question.

"Oh, I see. Decided to wear blue ones today, did you?"

"No. I usually wear brown ones. This is my real colour."

Her statement aroused my interest.

"Really? That's quite unusual, dark hair and blue eyes."

"Must be from my Gaelic ancestry," she said with an unusually warm and engaging smile. I'd never seen that before.

I was surprised, intrigued even. I wouldn't have expected Natalie even to have heard the word "Gaelic", let alone known what it meant. I felt the first stirring of suspicion that maybe there was more behind the image than I had previously given her credit for. She placed the piece of paper on my desk. It had a name and phone number written on it.

"Voice mail on the admin line this morning," she declared. "Wants you to ring him back."

I knew who it was from and that there was no urgency to reply.

"OK," I said.

Natalie didn't leave the office. She stood next to me for a few seconds, saying nothing. I looked up into her face again. She looked nervous.

"Can I talk to you for a minute?" she asked.

The untypical nature of Natalie's behaviour knew no bounds that morning.

"Of course," I said with undisguised surprise. "Have a seat."

There was a chair in the corner of the room which she pulled up to the front of my desk. She sat down and looked at me, clearly gathering the means to begin the sort of conversation to which I imagined she was unaccustomed.

"I'm a bit bothered about Nigel," she began tentatively. "Well, more than a bit really. And I'm bothered about lots of things, but they mostly have something to do with this business over Nigel. I saw him sitting in his car in the car park on Friday night. His car was next to yours. I suppose he came to see you, did he?"

I nodded.

"How is he?"

I pondered the question for a few seconds. I wasn't sure how much Nigel would want me to tell her, and I wasn't sure how much she had a right to know. I had the impression that she felt a strong sense of guilt in the matter, which surprised me given my previous impression of her, and I felt that telling her the whole story would only serve to strengthen that feeling. Would that represent justice, revenge or merely cruelty, I wondered. I decided to be kind and keep it brief.

"Well, he's a bit under the weather at the moment. His home life's not very wonderful, as you can imagine."

I thought she was about to cry but she held herself together. It seemed that her feelings of remorse went deep. And they triggered an outpouring that completed the total transition of my attitude towards her.

"I don't even know why I did it," she said after a pause. The look of frustration on her face seemed genuine. "I didn't actually like him, you know. I always used to try and keep him at arms length. I don't know why - he was a perfectly nice bloke - but there was just something about him. I didn't trust him, even though he'd never given me any reason not to. He made the odd comment, but nothing serious. He never touched me or asked me out or anything.

"But I felt like – well - like I didn't want to know him for some reason. Why the hell I went out with him that day and – well, you know - why I did *that*, I just can't figure out. Something just came over me, something I can't explain. I know I've got a reputation for being a bit loose, but it's not as true as everybody thinks. In fact, it's not true at all. Mrs Evans told me what he'd said about me to you the next day. 'A bloke for every day of the week' wasn't it? She's a prize bitch, you know. She really enjoyed telling me that.

"I'll tell you a secret, shall I? Nigel was the first man I've been with since my boyfriend left me six months ago. And, until then, he was the one and only. All this tarty front I put on – used to put on; this business is making me think again – it's all just an act. Sometimes I really want to put an old sweater and wellies on and go walking in the country. I want to have a dog and throw sticks for it, and paddle in the stream, and listen to the birds singing miles from anywhere."

She sighed and sniffed briefly, and then continued.

"Did you know I've got three A-levels?"

I tried not to show my amazement as I shook my head.

"No, you wouldn't. I only told them about my GCSEs when I applied for this job. By then I was into the 'image.' Having A-levels wasn't cool."

"So why do you do it?" I asked as she paused again. "Put on the front, I mean?"

She shrugged her shoulders and looked a little melancholy.

"That's how girls are now, isn't it? It's how we're supposed to be. I suppose I wanted to fit in. I was an only child and didn't make friends that easily. I used to read those pathetic lifestyle magazines and take the crappy TV adverts seriously, and they convinced me that I was ugly – and too skinny. At least, at first I thought I was too skinny. Then I believed I wasn't skinny enough. I became a bit bulimic for a while, but fortunately I got over that one without too much trouble.

"Then it was my hair and eyes. I noticed that you hardly ever see celebrities with dark hair and blue eyes. Most of them seemed to have blonde hair and blue eyes. I felt like a freak and was desperate to dye my hair. But I quite liked it the colour it was – it was about the only thing about myself I did like – so I decided to go for the easier option and get brown contacts instead; thought they'd go with my dark hair and make me look more sultry.

"And all the tarty dress was done to attract the attentions of men. Made me feel wanted, I suppose. I don't need it any more - I've decided. I never wanted ninety nine percent of them anyway. I used to find all that whistling and stuff repulsive. I felt like going over to them and saying 'when I want to have sex with a warthog, I'll go to the zoo and find a good looking one.' And yet I sort of enjoyed it as well in a strange, stupid sort of way. Does that make sense? Anyway, this business with Nigel has really had an effect on me. I feel rotten about it. Sick and rotten and guilty as hell."

She stifled a sob for a few seconds as I tried to come to terms with the new Natalie that was unfolding before me.

"Do you think there's anything I can do to help?" she asked eventually through bleary eyes. "Would it help if I phoned his wife or something, told her it was all a stupid mistake and it won't happen again?"

"Er, I don't think so," I said hurriedly. If Sarah felt antagonistic towards me, heaven knows how she would react to Natalie. "But can I just say this first of all, if it means anything to you? I happen to believe that the purpose of guilt is to point to some important lesson. Once you've learned it, there's no need to feel guilty any more; you can drop it. If there's nothing you can do about it, let it go.

"All the time I've known you, I've thought it a crying shame that you should have buried your natural good looks under a façade of paint and provocative clothing. I'm really glad you're seeing through it; long may it continue. Showing your true self to the world is very important in my opinion. They can take it or leave it as they wish. Stuff 'em. And, as you've said yourself, there's a lot more to you than you've cared to let on. Setting that free and letting it develop would be as good a reason as any to stop feeling guilty about something you can't change."

As I was speaking, she had her elbows on my desk and her chin was resting on top of her clasped hands. Her eyes fixed mine with an attentive stare. I decided that she really was very likeable. I couldn't resist a final, personal remark.

"Oh and, by the way, I think the combination of dark hair and blue eyes is very attractive. But then, I'm from a different generation, I suppose. My opinion probably doesn't count."

"Don't be silly," she said with a smile. "You're a really nice, genuine man. I've always thought so. I appreciate you saying that, honestly."

I smiled back, but then the serious nature of Nigel's predicament came to the fore again.

"As for Nigel, well..."

I decided to tell her everything. I felt that she should be given a full and frank appraisal of the facts, however distressing. I felt she'd earned it.

I began by asking her if she knew about the talisman. She did, she said. Nigel had joked about it when they went out that lunchtime. She clearly found the recollection unpleasant.

And had he told her about the curse that was supposed to be attached to it? No, she said. She looked a little shocked at that revelation. I told her the whole story, starting with Paddy's experience in Belfast and finishing with my abortive attempts to find an antidote for the curse.

"So, unless you know of anyone with the knowledge of how to lift curses, I don't think there's anything you can do."

Her look of mild interest had changed to one of horror when I related the part about Nigel's nightmares and his convictions regarding Sarah's pregnancy.

"God," she said with genuine feeling. "Poor bloke. That must have been horrible." She sat staring at the desk for a while, and then said wistfully "Pity you can't talk to my great grandmother. She's a real legend in the family for knowing all about ghosts and leprechauns and curses – all that sort of thing."

"Is she?" I asked, more out of politeness than any real belief in the possibility of a solution. "So why can't I talk to her?"

"She lives in a remote cottage, somewhere in Ireland. I've only met her once, when I was a kid.

We went for a holiday over there and looked her up. That's where I get my Gaelic blood from, my mother's side of the family. Mum was born in Ireland."

"Isn't she on the phone?"

"Dunno. If she is, we've never phoned her. I could try and find out I suppose."

Having drawn a complete blank on the subject myself, I decided that there could be no harm in following any possibility, however slight. I said as much, and Natalie seemed energised at the prospect of doing something positive that might alleviate Nigel's woes. I didn't share her optimism but was glad to see her feeling better. And energised she certainly was. She was back in my office ten minutes later, brimming with cheerful vitality.

"Right, I've phoned mum," she said brightly. "Threw her completely. 'Why are you suddenly interested in your great grandmother, dear? You've only met her once.'"

Natalie's imitation of her mother's apparently gentle Irish lilt was impressive. She continued.

"I made up some excuse about being interested in family history. Come to think of it, it's not an excuse really. Suddenly, I *am* interested in family history. That's good, isn't it?

"Anyway, she knows that great granny's not on the phone. Grandma, that's mum's mum, is always complaining that she can't ring her, and that's a problem 'cos grandma lives in Galway, but her mother still lives in Donegal where the family came from originally.

"I asked her if she knew great granny's address and she said she didn't, not exactly anyway. She always sends the Christmas card to grandma's address because that's where great granny spends Christmas every year. But they must know *where* she lives, even if they don't know her full address, because we went there when I was a kid, like I told you. And she can't have moved, or else grandma would have said so.

"Anyway, I let mum off the hook for now; she was getting a bit bewildered. But I'll wheedle it out of her or dad tonight, all innocent like."

She looked triumphant. I had just about managed to follow the logic of her breezy account but was a little confused as to its practical value.

"So what good will that do us, if we can't phone her?"

"Well, we'll just have to go and see her, won't we?"

"What! Go all the way to Ireland without phoning her first? She mightn't have a clue about lifting curses. She might have gone out for the day. She might be too senile to even know who you are. It's a ridiculous idea."

"Why?"

"Because it's not worth the risk."

"It is to me," she said, obviously taken aback. And then she turned a little petulant. "Oh well, I'll just have to go on my own then, won't I?"

"Oh come on Natalie, don't be silly."

"I'm not being silly. I thought you wanted to help Nigel."

"I do, but there are limits."

"No there aren't. If you won't come, I'll go on my own. If she's out for the day, I'll just have to hang around until she comes back. And there's no reason at all to think she's senile. That's just prejudice."

Emotional blackmail! So much for the reformed Natalie. But then I began to wonder whether she might be right. Should I be setting limits? It wasn't as though I

58

couldn't afford it, and my free time was hardly replete with meaningful activity. She stood and stared at me with a stern expression, defying me to take the right course or back out and be thought a wimp. I didn't want to be thought a wimp. Her eyes burned with that brand of Celtic fire that is peculiar to the women of Ireland. I hadn't seen *that* in her before, either. I convinced myself that she was probably right and made the decision on the spot.

"OK. Why not? When do you want to go?"

She looked pleased, or was it just smug? The chameleon that was Natalie was tossing my perception of her from pillar to post with its ever-fluctuating array of new colours. A sense of bemused wonderment began to take hold as it dawned on me that she, of all people, was taking charge of my affairs. It felt like the earth's axis was tilting. Never mind, I thought; an adventure is an adventure, whoever happens to be steering the ship.

"How about this weekend? The sooner we get it sorted, the better. Are you doing anything?"

I smiled at her with amused resignation and shook my head.

"Probably not."

"Right then. Overnight sailing on Friday. I'll book the tickets; you can pay me your share later. Whose car shall we take?"

"Mine. It's bigger and I'm a nervous passenger."

"Fair enough."

Her smile changed again to one that seemed to say "Aren't we doing well? Nice to meet you at last." Or was I just seeing my own feelings reflected there? I thought not. And at least I'd made one of the decisions, so the concept of team effort wasn't entirely dead.

She must have spent the rest of the morning getting on with her work, since I didn't see her again

59

until lunchtime. At one o'clock she came back to my office bearing a plastic box.

"Are you going out for lunch today?" she asked.

"No. I've got it with me."

"Me too. Can I eat it in here?"

"Of course. I'm ready for mine as well. I'll join you."

"Good. I'll give you the arrangements for the weekend while we eat."

We settled into our respective lunches, and even shared certain items that the other didn't have. I wasn't used to sharing; I hadn't had much practice. But it felt good. Natalie said that she had been searching the internet to get the cheapest sailing.

"There's one that leaves Holyhead at 2.30 and gets into Dublin Port at 5.45. I reckon it should take about two and a half hours to get to Holyhead so, if we leave at eleven, we should be in plenty of time. Agreed?"

I nodded.

"Good. I haven't booked cabins – thought we should save the expense. We can snatch a couple of hours in the lounge or somewhere. Is that OK?"

"Absolutely."

"Right. You'll pick me up at my house at eleven o'clock then? I'll get the directions to great granny's house off dad tonight."

She gave me her address and we spent the remainder of the lunch break discussing such trivia as how long we should wait if great granny was out, who would acquire a road map of Ireland and whether the crossing was likely to be rough at that time of the year. Before she went back to her own office, she told me how much she was looking forward to the trip and, if truth were known, I was becoming a little excited at the prospect myself.

I had the feeling that this was only the start of something much bigger. I hadn't yet felt the germinating seed of significance that was to take root as Natalie grew and blossomed in my life, but it occurred to me that the emergence of her truer, deeper nature might need something of a guiding hand to help it on its way, to smooth out some of the rough edges and fill in countless gaps that had undoubtedly been left by her insistence on paddling in the shallows for the past few years.

I knew I had no right to presume the position of mentor or guide in her life, and so I saw it as being akin to the duty of a midwife. The child, or so I perceived it, was fully formed and forcing its way out anyway. My job was merely to help it avoid the pitfalls along the way. And it struck me that there was probably nobody else available. Her parents, according to her description, were "nice" people but not particularly deep; and what few friends she had belonged to the clubbing and binge-drinking set. The opportunity to contribute to her greater development seemed like one of those responsibilities that life sometimes puts in front of you. And, I must admit, it was a boost to my ego too.

Natalie had lunch with me every day that week. She talked openly and enthusiastically, and I learned much about her upbringing and the influences that had shaped her attitudes to life. In return, she listened to my stories of the many and varied experiences that had informed my own beliefs and views. On such occasions she afforded me the rapt attention that a pupil might give to a teacher; though it would be wrong to take the comparison literally. It was neither as formal nor as profound as that. My ego wasn't quite *that* boosted.

We talked of cultures ancient and modern, the meaning, purpose and conduct of life, the question of God, and the place of formalised religion in the general scheme of society. To my surprise, as if my bag of surprises were not full to the brim already, she indicated that she had already started to understand how the system of control by global capitalism works, and how the myth of democracy keeps the masses on both sides of the development divide well and truly enslaved. She agreed with me that the system would inevitably collapse one day, forcing the human race - at least in the so-called "developed" world - to grow up and reorganise its priorities.

In particular, however, and with the imperative of current events very much in mind, we talked of talismans, curses and the semantics of luck. My previous sense of astonishment faded inexorably as she repeatedly endorsed my new belief that she was infinitely more than her previous show of cheap superficiality had indicated.

Throughout our talks, the role of leader had, as I expected, generally fallen on me; but I was constantly reminded that such a role required the willingness to take, as well as the capacity to give. By the time I picked her up at eleven on Friday night we had become equal partners in an adventure that would greatly alter the rest of our respective lives.

Chapter 5

When I stopped the car outside a tidy, semi-detached house at five to eleven on Friday night, I saw that Natalie was waiting at an upstairs window. She waved to acknowledge my arrival, so there was no need to knock. I saw the downstairs curtains pulled apart and the silhouettes of two apparently middle aged people look out in my direction. I assumed them to be her parents. The curtains closed again and, moments later, the front door opened and Natalie came hurrying down the path carrying an overnight bag. She opened the passenger door, threw the bag on the back seat, climbed in and began locating the seat belt.

"Go on then, drive," she said before it was even fastened. I duly obliged.

"What's the hurry?" I asked.

"My parents are a bit – how can I put it – old fashioned. They got used to me acting the part of prize bimbo because they knew it was just on the surface, but they wouldn't be best pleased at me spending a whole weekend with a man over twice my age. I told them I was going to Ireland with a girlfriend. I feel bad about it because, believe it or not, I don't like lying. I'll clear it all up when the job's done, but I didn't want the hassle of defying them if they tried to stop me going. I hoped they wouldn't see you in the dark and they mustn't have; they didn't say anything when I came out."

"Did you remember the directions and road map?" I asked.

She turned to look at me but said nothing. I looked back. Her head was slightly lowered and one eyebrow was raised.

"OK," I said, and chuckled. "Sorry."

The drive to Holyhead was uneventful and, for once, we talked mainly of trivial matters that would hardly warrant description. There were also long periods of silence, and it was after one such interlude that Natalie suddenly asked me

"Have you told Nigel about this trip?"

"Not exactly," I replied. "I felt I ought to call him and tell him that I was following a 'lead.' I didn't want to spell out the details, though. I didn't want to raise his hopes. I didn't want to mention your involvement either."

"How did he sound?"

"Pretty much the same. The dreams stopped after the tenth, apparently; but Sarah's still acting strange and the business of the pregnancy is still firmly rooted in his mind. In the end he just said 'thanks' and put the phone down on me."

She looked away from me, and there was a strangely ominous tone in her voice as she said

"I've got a bad feeling about this trip. Well, the whole business really."

"Oh?" I exclaimed with some surprise. "You were the one who really wanted to do it."

"I know. I still do," she said, turning to face me briefly and then looking away again. "I still think we need to do it, and I'm still quite excited about going. But, for some reason, I've had this sinking feeling all day today. A feeling that we're going to learn something interesting, some angle that we don't know about yet. But I don't think it's going to help Nigel. And, this is the worst bit, it felt like I suddenly didn't want to help him. I kept thinking about that lunchtime and it revolted me. I suppose I'm just a bit nervous and paranoid. The whole thing's probably just a fear of failure or something."

She looked at me again and I glanced back. She smiled, sadly I thought.

"Oh well," she said, "we'll probably know by this time tomorrow, eh?"

And then she laid her hand on my arm and I realised that it was the first time that there had been any physical contact between us.

"I'm a part of this problem," she continued. "I've got responsibilities. But you haven't. Thanks for being such a pal."

"No need for thanks, for pete's sake. I do feel a part of it, obviously. It was me Nigel came to for help. And, don't forget, it was me who gave him the talisman in the first place. Anyway, I like adventures."

She squeezed my forearm and, as far as I recall, we made the rest of the journey in silence.

When the formalities of checking in and boarding were completed, we went up to the lounge and Natalie produced a selection of welcome snacks that she had prepared at home. Having lived alone for most of my adult life, I found it comfortable to have someone taking care of my needs for once. I bought the coffees and we enjoyed the most agreeable of late suppers.

The night drive must have tired me more than I thought. I was surprised to be woken by a jolt as a rogue wave slammed into the ship's hull. I pulled myself up from my slouched position and looked at my watch. It was 4.30. Natalie was not in her seat and was nowhere to be seen in the quiet lounge. Assuming that she had probably gone to the loo, I decided I would take the fresh sea air to revive my torpid senses.

I donned my coat and went out to face the bracing wind on the observation deck. I closed my eyes briefly as a burst of spray hit them, and then opened them to see that Natalie was standing at the most forward point, leaning on the guard rail. There was a heavy swell on the sea that was big enough to make even the well-stabilised ferry pitch and roll, and the cold air smelt fresh and salty. I walked unsteadily forward to join her.

"Hello," she said as I nudged her elbow. "Awake then?"

"Just about."

"Look at that," she said with obvious enthusiasm. "The Holy Ground."

The sky ahead of us was lightening over a landmass that was obviously the east coast of Ireland. I smiled inwardly as I remembered that it was less than a week since I had been surprised that she knew the word "Gaelic." And now she was using soubriquets. I had heard the expression before.

"So they say. Won't be long before we'll be driving across most of it. I just hope it won't be a wild goose chase."

She looked at me with a quizzical frown.

"What?" I asked.

"Oh, just a bit of a coincidence. Did you know that, in Ireland, the term 'Wild Geese' is associated with the republican movement. It's used in various ways, apparently. It generally refers to displaced people, like those who went to America during the potato famine; but it came to be associated with freedom fighters. You hear it sometimes in Irish rebel songs."

"There's no end to your capacity to amaze me, is there?" I said.

"I've always been interested in Irish culture and history," she continued. "But I didn't know until the other day that great granny's uncle was an IRA man. He was involved in the Easter Rising and got himself shot by the British. Mum told me when I said I was coming over here. I asked her why she'd never told me before and she said that it's not the sort of thing you talk about in England. The IRA aren't exactly flavour of the month, are they?"

"No, we call them terrorists."

"Well, they are, aren't they? They kill innocent people. Or, at least, they used to."

"Yes they did, but you must have noticed how hypocritical we are on that subject. When people trying to throw off control by a foreign power are on our side, we call them 'freedom fighters' or 'The Resistance.' When they're on the other side we call them terrorists and murderers.

"The history books don't talk too much about the thousands of women and children who died in British concentration camps during the Boer War; or the thousands of unarmed civilians who were gunned down by the British army at Amritsar; or the episode in Croke Park, somewhere just the other side of those hills, back in the 1920's, when the Black and Tans opened fire on the crowd to teach the damn Paddies a lesson.

"It's the same with the Americans now. Remember Afghanistan? Every atrocity by the Taliban was greeted with howls of 'murderers' and 'cowards.' They seemed to forget that they'd trained those people to do the same to the Russians less than twenty years earlier. And what about the Second World War? We were happy enough to bomb thousands of German civilians as a legitimate weapon to 'spread terror.' The death toll at Dresden was at least 35,000, probably a lot more. And they were happy enough to do the same to us."

"But we were at war with Germany."

"The IRA was at war with us. And, let's face it, you can make a good case for saying they had a right to be."

"Suppose so," she said reluctantly. "But I still think it's wrong to hurt innocent people."

"Of course it is," I replied. "It's disgusting, obscene. I'm not excusing what they did. I just think we should be a bit less bloody pompous about it and accept that we're happy enough to sanction the same thing when it suits us. And, as far as the IRA's concerned, we created the situation that produced all those horrors in the first place."

"So do you believe in revenge then?"

I realised that I'd spent too much time on my soap box. I knew I had a tendency to run on a bit once I'd got the bit between my teeth. I felt that I should change the emphasis to something more general and objective.

"Not as a conscious act, no. I think it's pointless; it just perpetuates the misery. But I do believe in karma: that every action has an equal and opposite reaction that bounces back to you one day."

She stared at the approaching coastline and looked thoughtful.

"I've heard of that," she said. "I think I believe it too. It's what's bothering me at the moment. I keep feeling, for some reason, that something like that is what's going on in this business with Nigel."

"Why?"

"Don't know, just a feeling."

We both went quiet for a while and then made our way back to the lounge. When the announcement came to return to the car, we settled ourselves in and she gave me the route directions.

"It's easy enough. There are two ways we could go but the most straightforward is to take the N4 all the way to Sligo, then take the N15 to Donegal Town. Then we head west on the Killybegs road and take a left turn to Doorin Point. But I'll tell you more about that when we get there."

We disembarked at six fifteen and spent three delightful hours crossing the Emerald Isle from one coast to the other. We said little of any consequence during the drive, except to point out to one another odd little sights that caught our respective attentions. There were plenty of them, and the time passed quickly. We turned north to complete the final leg that would bring us to Donegal Town. As we passed between the first of the houses, I said

"I'm hungry. Let's have breakfast first."

"Oh no, let's go straight there."

This was a small test, but one that was easily mastered.

"Certainly not," I insisted, comfortable to be reasserting some control over my own affairs. "I'm driving and I'm hungry. Breakfast."

"OK," she said, and smiled that happy-to-know-you smile again.

We found a tea shop near The Diamond in the town centre. As we revelled in the delights of hot food and coffee, she gave me the final piece of the route.

"According to dad, you take the Killybegs road out of the town – that's this one isn't it? Right. Then there's a left turn about two or three miles out, signposted Doorin Point. You take that road and he thinks it's a mile or two down there on the left. He said it was a red and white painted croft and it's called Buncrana."

At ten thirty we were driving slowly down the appointed road and I was struck by the familiarity of the landscape. It reminded me of parts of Northumberland, where I had once lived, and also of Galloway in south west Scotland. The hedgerows and fields were unkempt but not, I felt, uncared for. I knew that the Irish had a great fondness for the land and didn't tend to treat it as a mere commercial commodity as we do in England.

The ground that made up the fields was uneven, as though it had only recently been claimed from harsh nature; and it was dotted here and there with wispy, isolated trees and gorse bushes. It occurred to me that they would look beautiful in early summer when the flowers were out. Scruffy sheep wandered lazily about and stopped to watch us as we drove slowly by.

Within minutes we saw a small croft by the side of the road. The house walls, the boundary walls and those of the small outbuilding to the side were all whitewashed. The wrought iron gate was also white, but the roofs and a few trimmings stood out in glorious, pillar box red. The sign to the side of the gate read *Buncrana*. Suddenly, I felt nervous. Natalie did too; she said so. I pulled the car off the road and parked close up to the gate.

"I never asked you," I said. "How old's your great granny?"

"Eighty next birthday," she replied.

"Mm, that's young for a great grandmother."

"I know. There's a story behind that. I'll tell you later."

"And what's her name?"

"Mary Molloy. Very Irish, eh?"

We got out of the car and started to open the gate. I began to wonder, for the first time oddly enough, just how we would broach the subject of curse-lifting with the old lady. My dealings with older people had been sadly limited and, prejudice or not, I still feared that she might not be entirely *compos mentis*. As the gate swung open, so did the front door and a handsome elderly woman with a magnificent mane of silver-white hair stood smiling at us. Her upright stance, warm smile and searching eyes dispelled my baseless fears immediately. I saw, for the first time I think, that captivating combination of grace and wisdom that only really comes with the experience of age.

"Natalie," she said, with a gentle power in her voice that still seemed out of place in a body of such advanced years. "Will you just look at yourself, now? How beautiful you've grown. And how lovely to see you."

Chapter 6

It seemed that somebody must have given the old lady forewarning of our intended visit. Natalie and I looked at one another in amazement. We quickened our stride towards the door and my companion asked the obvious question

"How on earth did you know who I was?"

"Oh, that's not so difficult," she said with the sweetest of smiles and a diamond-sharp glint in her eyes. "I had a premonition this morning that I was about to receive a visit from one of my family. I do, you know; get premonitions, that is. And you do look so very much like my own dear mother, God rest her. You couldn't be anybody else, now, could you?"

I was impressed. It appeared that Mrs Molloy's legendary reputation might be justified. The two women embraced warmly and then I was introduced as "David, a colleague and dear friend" who had something of great importance to ask her. Mrs Molloy frowned at me in a show of mock gravity, but then smiled again and said

"Well now, I'm sure that your business is of *very* great importance but, first of all, it would be no more than due and proper for us to catch up on family business. I'm sure you will agree, Mr...?"

"Lymer - David Lymer. I prefer 'Dave'."

"I'm very pleased to meet you, Mr Dave. You must both come in and take breakfast. You will excuse me for not joining you, but I take mine early. I still rise at six, you see. I can't get used to the fact that I haven't to milk the cows any more, even though I haven't done it for at least twenty five years."

She giggled like a schoolgirl and continued to hold one of Natalie's hands warmly between both of hers. Then she turned and walked into the house and we followed. Natalie explained that we had already breakfasted but we both agreed to take tea. We were directed to a comfortable armchair each and I took in the scene.

Apart from the modern, widescreen television set in the corner, everything else was comfortably old. The carpet square covering the quarry tile floor, the pre-war furniture, the ornately decorated crockery on the dresser, and the sundry ornaments – many of them family heirlooms no doubt – all spoke of a bygone age and reminded me of my own grandmother's house when I was a child. We waited as Mrs Molloy filled a kettle and placed it on the hob of the old range that stood on one wall of the living room.

"I see you still use the old methods, great grandma," said Natalie.

"I do indeed, dear. But, first of all, I would prefer it if you did *not* call me 'great grandma.' It makes me feel as though I am about to go to my maker, and I don't feel quite ready for that yet. I would rather you called me Mary. I know it is not strictly correct but, at my age, I feel entitled to dispense with formalities. And yes, I do prefer 'the old methods' as you put it. Can you tell me where there is a better smell anywhere on God's earth than the scent of a turf fire? Or any light more warm and comforting than an oil lamp? I will admit, I suppose, that it is very nice to get my water from a tap; and the electricity is useful for some things, like the radio."

"And the TV," offered Natalie, nodding towards the nearly new set that shouted its incongruous modernity from the corner.

"Oh that thing," replied Mrs Molloy dismissively. "Your grandmother bought me that a year or two ago. I've tried to watch it several times, so I have, but it was full of silly nonsense and I lost patience with it."

"Don't you find it a window on the outside world?" I asked.

It was the first time I had spoken except to introduce myself at the door. The words sounded stilted and academic, too formal for the cosy informality of a traditional Irish croft. I expected Mrs Molloy to scowl, and so she did.

"Yes, indeed it is," she replied sternly. "That's the problem. It seems the outside world is becoming stranger and stranger by the day. Frankly, I would rather do without it."

I offered my honest concurrence, and then Mrs Molloy asked Natalie how her mother was. That began a whole hour of family trivia and reminiscences, most of which was of only passing interest to me. She did turn directly towards me at one point to tell me that it was "a curious fact" that the women in the female line had all, "for generations longer than anyone can remember," had their first child at the age of twenty, and the first child had always been a girl. Natalie told me it was what she had been referring to earlier, and her great grandmother asked her

"Won't you be twenty yourself in another few months dear?"

Natalie looked embarrassed and said that she would be sorry to be the one to break the tradition.

"To be honest, Mary, I don't find young men very attractive really. I couldn't imagine marrying one of them – at least, none that I've met so far anyway. They're all so

74

immature. It was probably different in your day."

"Oh, I'm not so sure about that, now," came the reply. "I know what you mean, though. But then, we none of us know what the future has waiting for us, do we?" And I swear that she looked at me with eyes that seemed to say "actually, *I* do, and it's not what you think."

I put the impression down to an effect of the old lady's undoubted charisma and settled myself to more family trivia. I knew that I would have to curb my impatience. It was evident that Mrs Molloy lived, in her mind at least, in old Ireland where the modern preoccupation with pace was, and still is to some extent, less important than regard for human values and the personal touch. I respected that and was happy enough to make the effort – for a while at least. My tolerance became sorely tested, however, when the photo album was brought out. How long would this take, I wondered. I really did want to get the business concluded and get back to Dublin for the night sailing.

Natalie joined her great grandmother on the sofa and took the large, old book onto her lap. They began with the most recent pictures at the end and worked forward through the leaves, travelling back in time as they did so. Mrs Molloy offered me more tea which I declined.

"You will excuse us for a while longer, won't you?" she asked me graciously. "It's such a long time since I've had the opportunity, or the wish for that matter, to show this to anybody."

"Of course," I said, trying to attune myself to the mood of the moment and be gracious in return.

Natalie flicked through the pages, smiling every so often and asking pertinent questions. Her interest was obviously genuine and there was nothing I could, or should, have done to disturb her enjoyment of the saunter back through her family's history.

And then, suddenly and dramatically, her eyes widened and her mouth fell open. She laid a hand on one of the pictures and began to look increasingly distressed. Her breath quickened and a look came into her eyes that could have been fear or panic. Mrs Molloy stopped speaking and looked hard into Natalie's face. Natalie looked back and her expression changed to one of horrified realisation. It was the look of someone who had just been told a terrible secret. Her great grandmother gently removed her hand from the photograph and took the album from her. She laid it, open at the same page, on the arm of the sofa and said

"You obviously have the gift dear. I thought you probably would have. I'll get you some water; you'll soon be right again."

When Mrs Molloy had left the room, Natalie looked at me and pointed to the album.

"Look at that picture," she said weakly. "The one on the right hand side."

I went over, picked up the album and looked at the photograph. My reaction was not as openly dramatic as hers, but my sense of astonishment was still profound. It was a very old, black and white photograph, obviously taken in an urban photographer's studio. The sepia-tinted print was in excellent condition, though, and the image was crisp and clear. It showed a group of five people, posing self-consciously in a cheaply neo-classical setting, typical of those used by Edwardian photographers.

Sitting in the centre was a handsome woman of around thirty or so, with one arm around the waist of a young girl standing to her right. Behind her left shoulder were two young men, probably in their late teens. They stood with their bodies facing each other, their thumbs caught cockily under their lapels

76

and their heads turned proudly towards the camera. On the other side of her was an older man, perhaps in his early forties, with a mane of wild hair, reclining easily against a short, Corinthian column. What was so shocking was that three of the characters were immediately recognisable.

The child was the image of Natalie. The face, the body shape and the long dark hair were unmistakeable. And the two young men standing behind the seated woman's shoulder bore more than a passing resemblance to Paddy and Nigel. Apart from the difference in hairstyle and the fact that the "Nigel" character had a moustache, I would have said that they were nearly identical. The other two members of the ensemble bore no resemblance to anyone I knew personally, but it was remarkable that the third man was clearly much bigger than the other two and had a rough, weather-beaten sort of face that was a long way short of handsome. I had to wonder whether it just coincidence that he fitted the description of the man in Nigel's dream? I said nothing as I stared uncomprehendingly at the picture, but looked back at Natalie as Mrs Molloy re-entered the room with a glass of water.

"Drink this now dear," she said in a comforting, motherly sort of voice. "It is the best antidote. Strong psychic experiences can be very draining. I should know. You picked up some strong impressions from that photograph, didn't you?"

Natalie nodded but said nothing, and Mrs Molloy stroked her hair fondly. I felt I needed an explanation. I was conscious of the fact that my interest might be taken as impertinence, but asked the obvious question without hesitation.

"Mrs Molloy, who are the people in this picture?"

She looked across at me with a sad but tolerant expression.

"Am I right in thinking that this might have some connection with the reason for your visit?"

Either she had a deceptively quick mind for one who was so avowedly unworldly, or her psychic faculties were at work again.

"Quite possibly," I replied.

"Very well then. Come over here."

I went and sat next to her on the arm of the two-seater sofa. Natalie continued to drink her water on the other side. Mrs Molloy held out her hands and I gave her the album which she placed on her lap.

"It is a sad story this picture tells," she began. "My mother told it to me when I was about – oh, I don't know, probably about your age Natalie. It was taken in 1915, the year before the Easter Rising.

"The young girl is my mother, Brigit, aged 10. (You can tell how I knew who you were, can't you dear?) The older woman is her mother, my grandmother. This man," she said, pointing to the "Nigel" figure, "is her mother's brother, Liam O'Flynn. This man..." she pointed to "Paddy" "...is Liam's best friend, Patrick Callaghan. The brute of a man leaning on the pillar was called Donal McGuire. He was mother's stepfather – her own father had been killed a few years earlier in a farming accident. Mother said she was always a little frightened of him; though not with any real cause, she said, because he was always very gentle towards her. But she said that she loved Patrick best because he was so gentle and loving and kind. She wanted him to be her uncle as she didn't much care for her real uncle, Liam.

"Anyway, one night, something terrible happened. Liam was a member of the IRB – that's what the IRA used to be called, you know - and so was Donal. The whole family knew about it, though mother said she didn't really understand anything about that sort of thing at the time. Patrick, however, was not. It

78

seems he was just not inclined towards violence, no matter what the cause. Liam used to mock him openly and my mother disliked him, her uncle that is, all the more for it.

"So, this particular night – it was around the time of the Rising, shortly afterwards I think she said – Liam and Donal had been out on some sort of a mission, no doubt involving killing or burning or some such thing. They had been spotted and were being chased through the streets by the RIC or the army, or somebody in authority, when they ran into an alleyway and bumped into Patrick walking home from the pub.

"Liam was still carrying his gun and Patrick had the presence of mind to snatch it off him, saying that he was going to throw it into the river to dispose of the evidence. He put it into his pocket, but never got as far as the river. He was caught still carrying the weapon and was arrested, tried and sentenced to be executed. He was such a true friend to Liam that he never told the truth, but went to the gallows to save his friend.

"My mother said she was heartbroken and blamed her uncle for letting his best friend die in his place. I remember, when she was telling me, that she muttered something very dark-sounding in Gaelic, which I didn't understand. (Mother was fluent in Gaelic but I never learned it; it was not the done thing to speak Gaelic when I was growing up.) And I remember my father clearing his throat and spitting in the fireplace at the mention of Liam's name.

"Donal never spoke up either, of course. But then, I suppose he had to be loyal to a comrade and also protect himself. And Patrick, it seems, never gave Liam and Donal away to the British. Naturally, he protested his innocence, claiming that he had no idea how the gun came to be in his pocket. The court did not believe him, as I suppose they wouldn't. He went to his death bravely and, according to mother, was held in high esteem by the local brigade even though he had never been a member.

"Anyway, Liam and Donal laid low for a while. They stayed in the house most of the time and Liam became more and more quarrelsome and morose. Then, one day, he disappeared. Donal said that he had become frustrated at being cooped up, gone off to the pub and never returned. The story was that there were a couple of British agents in the town and they, knowing of Liam's membership of the IRB but having no evidence that would stand up in court, kidnapped and murdered him. It happened sometimes, apparently. There are even those who say it still does, but I wouldn't know about that now, would I? So, that is the story behind the picture."

"I heard that you had an uncle in the IRA who was shot by the British," said Natalie.

"No, dear, it was my mother's uncle. And it was only presumed that he had been killed by the British. It's what made the most sense of his disappearance."

I had listened intently to every word of Mrs Molloy's narrative and was trying fit pieces of it into the story of Nigel and the curse. It seemed that the most outrageous set of coincidences were being put before me which suggested an even more outrageous conclusion. I wanted to avoid accepting it. It was one of those situations when circumstantial evidence is at odds with the commonly accepted bounds of reason. I felt that the only course was to present the facts to Mrs Molloy and see what conclusion she came to. I went back to my own seat.

"Right," I began. "I have a story to tell you now, and one that seems to have some curious links with yours. Listen to this and tell us what you think."

I had a sudden thought and looked at Natalie.

"I'll have to tell her everything," I said apologetically. "Is that OK?"

"It'll have to be, won't it? You can't tell the story without that bit."

And so I told the whole story of the medallion and its apparent influence on the lives of Paddy, Nigel, Natalie and me. I left nothing out. When I told her of the astonishing similarity between the two men in the photograph and the two back home, her manner became grave and she nodded her head briefly. When I covered the incident involving Natalie's indiscretion, the younger woman blushed and the older one tutted in apparently feigned disapproval. By the time I got to the end, however, a look of genuine gravity had returned to the old woman's features. I deliberately avoided the temptation to make some speculative link between the people in the picture and those in my story. I thought I would wait and see what Mrs Molloy would have to say on that. Instead, I came straight to the point of our visit.

"So, do you think there's anything you can do about the curse?"

The palms of the old lady's hands were pressed together with her fingers touching her lips, and she remained looking at the floor in silence for some time. Eventually she looked up and said

"I've seen many strange things in my life and heard of many others, but this is certainly a match for any of them. There's something I must tell you, since it is what makes this situation so very extraordinary.

81

"My grandmother – the older woman in the photograph – died about fifty years ago and, of course, I went to her funeral. In those days, the deceased were laid out grandly in their coffin in the best room in the house, so that everyone could see them and pay their last respects.

"When I came to pay mine, I saw that she was wearing a medallion about her neck, and I remarked to my mother that the cross carved upon it wasn't straight. I didn't see the other side, of course. My mother said that she had been given strict instructions by her mother to ensure that the medallion was buried with her. She said it had been in Donal's family for many generations, but he had died some years before and his only remaining relations amounted to some distant cousins whose whereabouts nobody knew. The medallion, her mother said, had strange powers and it was important that it should not fall into the wrong hands. That was all she knew about it. She didn't take the story very seriously, but obviously honoured her mother's wish.

"Now, to come to your friend's dilemma. I have been a good Christian all my life, but there has always been a lot about the Roman Church that I didn't much care for. Some of their teachings and their practices always seemed wrong to me. And so, when I was old enough, I started to study everything I could find on the old Celtic Church – the one that was done away with at the Synod of Whitby.

"I read somewhere that they believed in reincarnation, and this seemed to me to make much more sense than notions of limbo, purgatory and the day of judgement – especially since the teachings seemed to vary according to which Pope was sitting in Rome at the time! So I came to believe in reincarnation too, and it has explained some of the things I have witnessed over the years.

"It seems to me that the explanation of your story is simple enough, even if it may seem far-fetched to you. The woman who gave the medallion to your friend Paddy was probably the reincarnation of my grandmother, repaying him for the favour he had done her brother Liam all those years ago. It is very rare for people to have such a clear remembrance of their previous lives, but I have heard that it happens sometimes. And somehow, by what means I really don't know, a train of events was set in motion so that her brother received a slice of the luck too. Only, in his case, his desires were less than honourable and he also failed to pass on the medallion. So the curse was invoked and he has suffered for it.

"The one thing I don't understand is how the medallion was physically removed from my grandmother's body and brought down to you through the years like that. Perhaps it was never buried with her. Perhaps the undertaker took a liking to it and removed it for himself, and then it came into the woman's possession through some accidental, or even pre-ordained, means. God really does move in mysterious ways, doesn't he?"

The explanation was the one that I had tried not to accept before Mrs Molloy trotted it out. Being a believer in Vedic philosophy, I had long been convinced of reincarnation. It had always struck me as irrational that people could believe in the persistence of spirit or consciousness after death, yet refuse to believe that the same "indestructible" spirit could have existed before the life of the body which it inhabited. I had also heard it said that the physical appearance of certain individuals is often very similar from one life to another. Nevertheless, I still found it hard to believe that such principles could be made manifest in so clear a way as this. The conclusion was both obvious and unbelievable in equal measure.

But then it struck me that such occurrences might be more common than we know. Maybe

83

Natalie and I had simply been afforded the rare privilege of seeing the process in action. Whether it was true or not, however, there was still the pressing problem of Nigel's dilemma to be addressed. I asked Mrs Molloy if she could remove the curse. She shook her head.

"I'm afraid not," she said gravely. "You see, either your friend – what was his name?"

"Nigel."

"Either your friend Nigel's dreams were just that, in which case the matter has already taken its course and is finished; or the dreams were something more, some strange working of a power that is beyond our comprehension, and his wife really does have a new life growing inside her. In that case, what would you have me do? Try to destroy that life? That would be murder, would it not?"

I had no option but to accept her logic and respect her principles.

"So Nigel will just have to live with the consequences then?"

"We all have to live with the consequences of our actions. That is only proper."

It seemed a little unfair to me that, if Nigel had brought the curse down upon himself, his only "action" had been an error of omission rather than commission. The "consequences" hadn't been invoked through his indiscretion with Natalie, but through his failure to pass on the medallion. I wondered whether it was the process of karma at work again – maybe the curse was repayment for allowing an innocent friend to die in his place. I was shortly to discover that the situation was more complex than that but, for the time being, I was content to accept the simple explanation.

The three of us went quiet for a while, and then Mrs Molloy looked at Natalie and spoke brightly again.

"Will you be taking your lunch with me today? It's a long time since I've cooked for my family." She turned to me and smiled. "And guests, of course."

But Natalie still looked pale and a little distressed.

"To be honest Mary," she said, "I'm not really up to eating at the moment. And we do need to get back to Dublin for the overnight sailing. I think I'd like to go and take the sea air at the bottom of the road for a while, if you don't mind. Clear my head a bit. The road does go to the sea, doesn't it? It looks like it does on the map."

"It does indeed dear. And I quite understand you not wanting to eat. A little of the sea air will do you good."

"Thanks. We'd better be off then. Thank you for the tea and all your time. I promise I'll come back and see you again before too long."

"Before you go," said Mrs Molloy, "I think you should take this to show to your friend Paddy. I have no doubt he will find it interesting."

She slipped the photograph out of its corner mounts and handed it to me. I promised to have a copy made and return the original to her. She told me to give it Natalie instead, who could either keep it or return it the next time she visited.

We took our leave of the old lady and drove off down the road until it faded into the rocky foreshore of Doorin Point. Natalie was opening her door before I turned the engine off. She sat with her legs out of the car for a few moments, breathing in the sweet salt air.

"Come on," she said gravely, "there's something I've got to tell you."

She walked off and left me to lock up the car. I followed and came up beside her as she stood staring at the sea. She looked forlorn, standing alone with her hands in her coat pockets. The day was grey but mild, and a gentle breeze stirred some wisps of her long hair. Apart from the lapping of the waves, silence reigned. And then she spoke.

"Tell me, how long did I have my hand over that photograph?"

"I don't know. Five seconds, ten maybe. Why?"

"Because it felt like half an hour. It was like one of those dreams where you see every detail and it seems to go on for ages. Then you wake up and realise you've only dozed off for a few seconds." Her look carried a hint of incomprehension as she continued. "What's the name they use for that skill some mediums are supposed to have, when you can pick things up from objects – psychically, I mean, like Mary said?"

"Psychometry."

"Right, well this was psychometry with a capital 'S'."

"'P' actually" I said, feeling immediately guilty for correcting her. She ignored the rebuke anyway.

"I saw everything. I became Brigit. I was in her body - watching, listening, and feeling. And I saw, and heard, and felt *everything*. It was horrible, loathsome, disgusting. Mary didn't give us the true story."

"Really?"

"Absolutely."

"Why not? Why would she lie?"

"She didn't lie. She told the story that had been given to her. It was her mother who lied – Brigit, the child in the photograph thirty years on. She couldn't tell her daughter the truth; it was too shameful I suppose - even though she had nothing to be ashamed of."

"So what is the truth?"

"What I saw."

"Which was?"

I was becoming intrigued and impatient, as well as feeling that I might need to be circumspect about Natalie's experience. The possibility of hallucination crossed my mind. Natalie took a few deep breaths of Atlantic air and then began the narrative.

"I was in the kitchen having breakfast, the morning after Patrick's arrest. I knew there was a bad atmosphere in the air, especially between the two men. The story of the previous night was being told to my mother and I was old enough to pick up what had happened.

"The two of them had, indeed, been escaping from the police. But they hadn't bumped into Patrick in the street. They'd run into a pub where they often drank, knowing that the landlord was sympathetic to the cause and would let them out the back way.

"Patrick was drinking at the bar. He was already drunk, and somehow I knew that drink was his big weakness – I suppose Liam did too. He'd gone there straight from work and had his tool bag with him. Liam spotted his opportunity and managed to slip the gun into the bag without being seen. Then he ordered two drinks, one for himself and one for Donal, ignoring Donal's pleas to be making good their escape. The police burst in through the front door and searched everybody. They found the gun in Patrick's bag and gave him a good beating before taking him away.

"As I listened, it became obvious that Donal was angry and disgusted that his brother-in-law could do such a thing. He said they should have tried to escape; it would have been more honourable. But Liam just smirked and said that Patrick was useless anyway and that it was about time he did something for the cause. Mother said very little. I had the impression that she was concerned for Patrick, but was even more worried that the police might be banging on the door at any minute to arrest her husband and brother.

"What Mary said about them lying low was true. And I certainly did hate my uncle Liam more than ever, but with more cause than Mary knows. Because that wasn't the end of it. Oh God, I don't know whether I can go through the rest of it. I still feel sick at the thought."

I waited patiently as she took another deep breath and looked up at the sky, as though searching for some strength or inspiration, or both, from a higher source.

"As Liam became more and more 'morose', as Mary put it, I saw him starting to look at me in a way that I'd never seen before and didn't understand. I thought it was just a look of hatred because he realised that I hated him so much.

"But then, one day, when mother and Donal were out shopping, I went up to my bedroom to practice my reading. I was sitting on the bed when Liam came in. The look on his face was the one I had come to see so often, only stronger. He undid the buckle on his belt and I thought he was going to thrash me. I began to feel scared. But he didn't take the belt out of the loops: he took his trousers off instead. And then his underpants. What I saw standing out from below his shirt filled me with horror and disbelief. I didn't know what to make of it, but I knew it was something horrible and threatening. Then he came over and pushed me back onto the bed, holding me down with one hand pressing on my chest, while he pulled my knickers off with the other.

"I felt terrified, confused and unable to breathe. He put both hands under my knees and lifted my legs, pulling them apart at the same time. I don't have to describe the rest, do I? You've got the gist haven't you? The pain, the fear, the disbelief: it was indescribable. I felt dizzy. I didn't understand what was happening. I could smell his horrible breath and see the sweat standing out on his forehead. When I screamed out, he put one hand over my mouth and I couldn't breathe again. And when it was all over, he told me that, if I said a word to anybody, he'd get all his friends to come in and do the same to me over and over again, every time my mother went out. Imagine that. And this was the man who looked exactly like Nigel. How do you think that made me feel?"

I didn't know what to say. Natalie was clearly distressed and I rubbed my hand across her back in a gesture of sympathy. She collected herself and continued.

"Anyway, when mother came home she called me from the bottom of the stairs. I was in a state of shock and didn't reply, so she came up to my bedroom. She saw the state I was in and asked me what was wrong. I still didn't reply. 'Are you ill,' she asked me, and all I could do was nod.

"She kept me in bed and called a doctor in. He took my temperature and came out with some waffle about me having the 'flu. He said I'd be fine in a few days. I didn't say a word in those few days; I was terrified I might let the cat out of the bag. And then mother told me that Uncle Liam had been called away to a meeting somewhere and would be gone for a few days.

"Suddenly, I felt safer and the dam broke. I told her everything and saw her grow more horrified as the story unfolded. She stood up without a word and pulled the bedclothes back. Then she lifted my nightie. I suppose there must have been some bruising there and some blood on the nightdress, because she let out a shriek and then turned away and started sobbing. I just sat there, feeling frightened again. I hated myself. I felt that I was the one guilty of causing my mother such distress. She pulled herself together, covered me over and went downstairs.

"I heard raised voices – both hers and Donal's – and I heard her sobbing again. Then there was silence. And then a bang as the back door slammed. I jumped up and looked out of the window. Donal was striding down the back yard towards the gate. He turned and looked up at me. I'd never seen such anger in his eyes. I thought he was angry with me. He went out of the gate and disappeared down the entry. He didn't come back that night and mother spent the whole evening holding me and rocking me until I went to sleep.

"The next morning, Donal came into my bedroom. I thought he was going to beat me and I was frightened again. But he didn't. He smiled and asked me how I was feeling. He sat down on the bed and told me that I should never be afraid of Uncle Liam any more. I would never see him again, he said; he'd made sure of that. He never did come back and I never knew what had happened to him. The story was put around that he'd been kidnapped and shot by the British and that was that."

I felt an instinctive need to massage the back of her neck as we stood in silence for some time.

"You think you're the reincarnation of Brigit, don't you?" I remarked eventually. She shrugged.

"Don't know. The sights, the smells, the feelings – they were all as real as a true memory. And I feel sure that the only other person Brigit ever told about her ordeal was her husband, when she got married. Probably why he spat in the fire at the mention of Liam's name. I just seem to know it, like that's a memory too."

It was my turn to take a deep breath and blow it out to join the wind. I was struggling to know whether to take the story seriously or not. The more I thought about it, however, the more it fitted the circumstances better than Mrs Molloy's version.

"If all that's true," I said eventually, "it seems that Nigel has two crimes to answer for."

"Exactly," said Natalie. "I suspect that Donal caught up with him and murdered him. Or maybe he just gave him a good beating and sent him packing, and Liam died some squalid death years later, somewhere far away. I don't know. Whatever happened, I suppose that was the crime against Patrick paid off. But there was still the crime against Brigit. What was Mary's phrase? 'Some pre-ordained means', 'some strange workings of fate.' I really think that I was that pre-ordained means. Perhaps I am the reincarnation of Brigit and was taking my revenge that day. You think revenge is a bad thing, don't you?"

"I don't see it as revenge," I said. "You didn't know any of this then. I'd prefer to think of it as the workings of karma. You were just the unsuspecting instrument."

"Maybe," she said, looking unconvinced. "But I said it was odd, didn't I, that I went out with him that day, even though I'd never liked him? It seems now that I was a woman with a mission. And maybe that's why I had such a low opinion of myself all those years and behaved like a tart."

I tried to find the right words to put her mind at rest but, as is often the case, they failed to come immediately. I suggested that we walk along the shore, which we did for a while in silence. The peace and serenity of the place seemed somehow like nature's balm, cooling and soothing the hot, frantic energies stirred up by all the terrible revelations of the past couple of hours. Eventually we went back to the car. My thoughts had cleared a little by that time and I offered her my honest opinion.

"Let's face it," I began, "we're never going to know whether you're the reincarnation of Brigit or not, are we? You might be; or then again, you might just happen to look very much like one of your ancestors. It's not unusual; I look a lot like my dad's father.

"But if you are, I think you should try to see it like this. You had a very terrible, traumatic experience once. I'm sure that sort of thing stays with a person – soul, spirit, whatever you want to call it – for a long time, until something comes along to exorcise it. Think of this as the catharsis to which you were fully entitled.

"You didn't go out with Nigel that day bent on revenge. You were following some sort of imperative that you didn't even realise was there. You're completely innocent. And look what this whole business has done for you. You've blossomed into the mature, decent, concerned, intelligent young woman that's been waiting to get out all along - probably the person Brigit would have been if dear Uncle Liam hadn't come along.

"And if Nigel really was Liam and is now getting his just desserts, that's fine too. I'm sure we all have to pay off our karmic debts some time. He probably messed up Brigit's life pretty seriously. Bad emotional experiences in childhood leave people with scars that affect their perceptions, relationships, abilities – everything – for the rest of their lives. If Nigel's life has got messed up, so be it. It's his fault, not yours."

Natalie said nothing. She was fiddling nervously with the heavily crumpled corner of a tissue that she had taken out of her pocket when we got into the car. We sat for a couple of minutes looking at the sea. She spoke suddenly.

"So you're really convinced about all this reincarnation stuff, then?"

I took the photograph out of the glove compartment where I had put it for safe keeping. I showed it to her and said

"Look at those two men. Can there really be any doubt?"

"I don't have any doubts," she said, looking deeply into my eyes. "I saw what happened a year after it was taken, remember? I even felt the pain, here."

She started to point to the relevant spot and then waved her hand about indiscriminately. Whether that was a gesture of embarrassment or a desire to push away the memory, I couldn't tell.

"I just want to know that you believe it, too," she continued. "I want to know that you believe *me*. And I want you to respect me. I've become very fond of you."

At that, she brought the pathetic little tissue up to her eyes and wept quietly for a few seconds. I put one arm around her shoulder, squeezed gently and said

"No problem with that; none at all."

She turned towards me, put her arms around me and cried gently on my shoulder for several minutes. Naturally, I allowed her whatever time she needed. And then, quite suddenly, she detached herself from me, sat upright on her seat and blew her nose in what remained of the tissue. She looked at me with red-rimmed eyes and smiled.

"What am I going to do with this?" she asked, holding up the small ball of sodden paper.

"Eat it," I joked. "Destroy the evidence."

She placed it on top of the dashboard.

"Souvenir," she countered. Then she fastened her seat belt, took another deep breath, exhaled sharply and said "I'm ready for lunch now. Take me to lunch, David. I'm buying."

It was a relief and a joy to see her back to her bubbly, assertive self. We drove back to Donegal, had lunch in the place we had found earlier and then explored the town for a couple of hours to wile away the time before we needed to drive back to Dublin. We finished the walk with a stroll through the ruins of the old abbey that stood beyond the harbour. Natalie wandered among the gravestones, stroking each of them in turn.

"Do you feel anything?" I asked her.

"Lots of things," she said. "But they're all jumbled up. I think I need to practice this – what's it called again?"

"Psychometry."

"Right - with a 'P'."

"If you get good at it, you could pitch a tent in the fair at Blackpool and make a fortune – telling fortunes."

"Don't think so," she said, looking wistful again. "I think I know what I'm going to do."

"What's that?"

"Come and live here. I feel it's where I belong. It would be like coming home. Do you know where the name Donegal comes from?"

"No."

"It's from the Gaelic 'Dun na nGall' and it means 'fort of the stranger.' Apparently it refers to the Vikings who first founded a settlement here. I looked it up before we came."

"That's interesting," I said. "Maybe that's how the medallion got here in the first place. I must admit, old Donal did look a bit like a Viking, didn't he? You could see him sitting in a longboat, sharpening his battle axe."

"He does, yes," said Natalie with half a smile. "That's history though, isn't it? I just think it's ironic: 'fort of the stranger', when I feel anything but a stranger here."

"Perhaps you don't have any Viking blood," I said. "I know what you mean, though. I feel oddly at home here, too. There is something comfortable about the place."

She was leaning easily against one of the Celtic-cross gravestones that stood on the estuary side of the abbey. She was stroking one of the rounded portions of it and looking at me with an intensity that made me sit up and wonder what it meant. The only word I can find to describe the look in her eyes is "knowing." It was as though she knew something that I didn't – something about my destiny perhaps. It was an optimistic look and it passed in an instant.

"Well," I said, "it's nearly five o'clock and the sailing's at nine fifteen. I think we should be heading off."

She agreed and we walked back to the car. As we drove through the town, she looked around at the buildings and muttered a promise to return soon. I thought it no more than a romantic whim at the time. It seemed like one of those promises that people make to keep in touch with acquaintances they've met on holiday. I should have known that Natalie was not the sort to make promises lightly. Natalie still had depths I hadn't seen yet.

Chapter 7

The return trip was uneventful. The ferry was busier than on the way out, and we were blessed with the presence of a group of rowdy young people whom Natalie regarded with amused tolerance. I just felt irritated. She pointed out a pair of provocatively dressed young women who were clearly flaunting their attributes for general consumption.

"Who do they remind you of?" she asked, smiling.

"I don't think I care to remember," I said. "I wonder if either of them knows what 'Gaelic' means." She punched me playfully on the shoulder.

We enjoyed little in the way of meaningful discourse for the first hour of the journey, partly because the general hubbub made talking uncomfortable but also, I think, because we had both had enough of high emotion and deep drama for one day. I felt the need to sit and muse on the outcome of the trip and so, I suppose, did Natalie. We did have one serious conversation though, when the rowdies had taken themselves off to the duty-free shop.

"We haven't discussed what we're going to tell Nigel," she began. "It was the reason for going over there, remember?"

"Could hardy forget it, could I? Though I'm not sure about the 'we.' It was me Nigel entrusted his problem with. It's me who's supposed to be finding an antidote for his curse. And it's me who'll have to tell him what we found out."

"What, everything?" she asked, frowning with doubt.

"I suppose so. Why not?"

"Well, the way I see it, he doesn't strike me as the type who's likely to believe in reincarnation. He might have got himself convinced about the curse because he's desperate. But reincarnation? And, if he did believe it, you'd be telling him what a shit he'd been and how he deserved it all. That would make him feel a whole lot better, wouldn't it? It's bad enough telling him you can't help him with his problem. Personally, I think you should leave it at that, apologise and leave all the other stuff out. It's not lying, is it? We really didn't find a solution to his problem, did we? Telling him the rest will just open another can of worms of one sort or another."

"Mm, don't know," I said. "I'm going to have to phone him tomorrow or Monday and arrange to meet him somewhere. I'll see how he is and play it by ear. How do you feel about Nigel now?"

It was a sudden change of tack, but one she seemed to have been expecting.

"Not sure," she replied without hesitation. "I was thinking about that during the drive back to Dublin. I know what he was once. I know what he did to me and to other people, and part of me loathes him for it. But he isn't that person now; he's somebody else. In this life he's been basically a decent bloke. Bit shallow, but generally OK. I'm struggling with that one. I don't fancy him coming back to work though, I have to say that. I'll find it very difficult to look into his eyes again. I think that's what changes least when you're reincarnated: the eyes."

"Windows to the soul," I offered.

"Anyway," she said, "it won't be for long. I'll be leaving soon, won't I?"

"Will you?"

"Of course. To go and live in Donegal."

"Oh, right, I'd forgotten that. You're serious then?"

"Absolutely. No doubts at all. It's where I belong."

"Fair enough." I was still not sure I believed it.

And then she went of to the bathroom for a wash and a change of clothes. I watched her cross the busy lounge with her overnight bag and realised that she only ever wore long skirts these days. The tight jeans, it seemed, were a thing of the past.

There was no need to sleep on the return trip. We arrived at Holyhead shortly after midnight and Natalie offered to drive home. I'd done all the driving up to that point and was happy to accept.

"You sure you're up to it?" I asked sympathetically.

"Up to it!" she replied sternly, and with that flash of Celtic fire that I'd seen once before.

"OK. Thank you," I said hurriedly. The flash of fire melted into the same smug smile, and I couldn't resist a friendly rebuke. "Paddy called you a 'minx', you know. I think he might have been right."

"So do I," she said. "Nice minx though." We both chuckled.

I dozed off several times during the long drive back to her house. I felt guilty, but Natalie didn't seem to notice. All the houses were in darkness when we drove down her street shortly after three o'clock. She stopped the car and said

"Oh God, I've just had a thought. I didn't tell them when I was coming back. I wasn't sure how things would go over there. The catch is probably down on the front door. Would you wait for a bit while I find out?"

She took her bag and made her way to the front door while I moved over into the driver's seat. I saw her put her key into the lock and take it out again. She walked back to the car.

"Thought so. How do you feel about an overnight guest? Save waking the folks up."

"The spare bedroom's full of junk" I said, "but you're welcome to the sofa".

"That'll do. I could sleep on a clothes line tonight."

We drove home to my house where Natalie made two mugs of tea while I fetched a couple of blankets for her makeshift bed. We sat down to drink them, she on the sofa and me in my usual armchair.

"You've taught me a lot over these last couple of weeks," she said.

"Have I? Maybe, maybe not. Perhaps Richard Bach was right." I was referring to a book I had lent her which explained, through the medium of a simple, entertaining fiction, the basics of Vedic philosophy. "Maybe I only reminded you of what you knew already."

Here we were again, surrounded by the serenity of extraneous silence, talking of deep and meaningful things. But it was late and I was tired. I finished my tea quickly.

"Time for bed," I said, getting up.

Natalie joked that I had less of a spring in my step than the redoubtable Zebedee. And then she did it again; she gave me another look that I had trouble understanding. And she got up too. She came towards me, enfolded me in a tight embrace and laid her head on my shoulder.

"You really are a bit special, you know. Thanks," she said softly.

Then she stood away from me, waved her hand in a small, childlike manner and said

"Night night."

I went to bed with a confused set of emotions, but fell asleep immediately. Natalie woke me up at eleven the next morning with a mug of coffee. She sat on my bed.

"Didn't know whether you preferred tea or coffee first thing," she said brightly. "Hope this is OK. But don't take too long about getting up, will you. It's about time I went home."

I drove her back to her house at lunchtime and offered to park around the corner, out of sight of her parent's twitching curtains.

"No need," she said. "They'll be OK when they hear the whole story. I expect dad will scoff, but mum'll be fascinated. She loves anything weird. I'm not sure I'll tell them absolutely everything, though. I think *I'll* play it by ear too."

When I pulled up outside her house, she gave me a kiss on the cheek and got out.

"Good luck with Nigel," she said, before shutting the door and walking briskly up the garden path.

I'd almost forgotten about Nigel. The problem now was how much to tell him. I gave the matter a lot of thought throughout Sunday afternoon and decided to lay all the facts on the table honestly, completely and without apology. That was my way. I felt that merely telling him that my mission to find an antidote to the curse had been a failure would just leave him feeling flat and dejected. I thought he should be told the whole story in the hope that he could make greater sense of what had happened. I hoped it would enable him to be more philosophical about it.

I knew that it would be risky, of course. It was difficult to know whether he would even believe the story and, if he did, how it would inform his perception of himself and his situation. The ability to be objective about one's own failings is sometimes difficult, even for philosophical people in ordinary circumstances. I had never seen Nigel as being that way inclined, and his circumstances were far from ordinary.

But I still believed it to be the right course. The truth must out, I thought. And if it hurt him, I could only regret the unfortunate necessity and rely on the old maxim that "truth is your ultimate defence." I rang his mobile number but there was no reply, so I left a voice mail message. I tried it twice more during the evening but the result was the same. I decided to call him from work the next day.

Chapter 8

It felt strange going back to the office on Monday morning. The weekend had been so full of drama, emotions and learning. I had been to a truly foreign country in that lonely lane, tucked away in a corner of the north west of Ireland. I had heard an extraordinary, violent story that I felt every reason to believe, and which I had no doubt was somehow responsible for creating and manipulating an extraordinary, modern denouement. I had come to know a remarkable young woman and was feeling the power of a heady, magnetic attraction to her, the nature of which was something I had never felt before.

Last Friday night was less than three days ago, and yet it seemed like an eternity. The prospect of seeing her again in the cold light of a busy and businesslike Monday morning was both thrilling and nerve wracking. I hoped that the magic between us would be undiminished, but I was realistic enough to suspect that it might prove to be an illusion. I had a vision of reaching out to catch a magnificent, multi-coloured soap bubble - only to see it disappear as soon as my fingers touched its gossamer surface.

I was not the first to arrive. The office door was open and I walked in, expecting to find the cleaner preparing to depart. I walked down the empty hall and called out. Receiving no reply, I continued to the small staff dining area towards the back of the building and that was empty too. I was about to go though into the kitchen which lay beyond it when Mrs Evans came out, carrying a mug of coffee. The look on her face was, as usual, cold as the chill October morning. She walked past me, heading back towards the hall.

"Morning Mrs Evans," I said politely.

"Did you have a good weekend?" she asked me curtly, without bothering to turn around.

It was clear that there was no real interest in her enquiry; she was merely returning the politeness for the sake of propriety. She was walking away from me and was just rounding the corner of the stairwell.

"He spent it with me, actually."

It was Natalie's voice, coming from the direction of the front door. I hurried around the corner in Mrs Evans' wake.

"It was great, wasn't it Dave?" she continued mischievously. Then she tripped lightly up the stairs and out of sight.

Mrs Evans paused only briefly and then walked on. She didn't turn around to look at me. I didn't need to see her face to know the set of her mouth and the undoubted look of disgust in her eyes. I smiled silently behind her back and went upstairs too. Natalie put her head girlishly around the door frame as I reached the top. She whispered loudly

"Sorry about that. Couldn't resist it."

I smiled broadly at her. It seemed that I had taken the bubble in my hands and, miraculously, it hadn't burst. And, when I reached my office and looked out of the window, I saw that Natalie's car was not in its usual place. It was at the bottom side of the car park, next to mine.

I rang Nigel's mobile number several times during the morning, but it went straight to voice mail every time. Either he was using it or it was switched off. By lunchtime I was surprised that he had not responded to the message I had left the previous day, and said as much to Natalie when she came in to have lunch with me. I told her of my decision to give Nigel the full facts and she just shrugged as she took a bite of her salad sandwich, trying to catch the pieces that were falling out of the side.

"Good weekend wasn't it?" she mumbled, when the sandwich and her mouthful of food were back under control. "I can't believe it's only forty eight hours since we were talking to Mary in her croft down that little lane."

"I know," I said. "Time seems to go haywire when you jump from the banal to the extraordinary and back again."

"Do you know, Dave, you do have a good way of putting things," she said with some enthusiasm.

I was about to say "do I really?" when I saw her look across at the office door. The expression on her face changed and she stopped eating. I looked in the same direction and saw a woman framed in the doorway.

She was about thirty, prim and well dressed in a lower middle-class sort of way. Her honey-blonde hair was immaculately styled and she was wearing just the right amount of expertly applied make up, so as to be presentable without being "obvious." Whilst not being beautiful, nor even uncommonly pretty, she was certainly good looking; and she had that confident, detached air typical of the well-heeled woman from the better class of suburb. Though I had never seen her before - and neither, I assumed, had Natalie - we both sensed immediately who she was.

"You're David, I believe," she said curtly.

I nodded.

"Can I come in and talk to you? I'm Sarah, Nigel's wife."

I looked at Natalie and she looked back. She got up immediately and gathered her lunch items together.

"I'll leave you to it," she said, and then walked out through the door giving Sarah only the briefest glance.

Sarah stood aside and looked more pointedly back. I invited her in and she took the place that Natalie had vacated. She looked uncomfortable sitting in the same seat, but there were no others.

"Is that her?" she asked.

I said nothing but only nodded in a way that was meant to look apologetic.

"Pretty young thing, isn't she? And not as tarty as I would have expected."

Her manner was calm and organised, but there were unmistakeable hints of malice, surprise and disappointment in her voice. I remained non-committal and merely shrugged.

"However," she continued, "it's not her that I've come to talk about. It's Nigel."

"How is he?" I asked. "I've been trying to call him."

"Yes I know. I picked up your message on his phone. He's not well, I'm afraid, not well at all."

I was stuck for an appropriate reply for a second, but she continued anyway.

"Before I come to that, though, I should say that I wanted to come and see you for a number of reasons. Firstly, I felt I should apologise for being so rude to you when you called. I wasn't myself at the time, you understand. I've calmed down since then and realised that it was a bit ridiculous to blame you for my predicament. I'm sure you had the best of motives for giving Nigel that good luck charm and, of course, I don't believe that it had anything to do with his behaviour anyway. I'm sorry."

"Don't be," I said. "I fully understand."

"Thank you," she said, with little enthusiasm. "Secondly, I gather you've seen him since those abortive attempts to call him at home. I suppose he told you how things have been between us for the last couple of weeks?"

"He did say a few things, yes."

"Well I want you to hear my side of the story, partly to set the record straight and partly since it might help to shed some light on his subsequent behaviour. When the facts of his present situation come out, I want it to be known that he might not be wholly to blame."

"What situation?" I asked.

"I'll come to that presently," she continued. "I'd like to start at the beginning if you don't mind."

She paused briefly to gather her thoughts.

"You see, there was something Nigel didn't know until two days ago, something I hadn't told him. Had I done so at the outset, things would probably be very different. That's why I feel guilty, you see?"

I felt puzzled and it must have showed.

"No, of course you don't. I'm sorry, let me start again."

She paused again and I sensed that her air of cool, controlled detachment was a front that she was struggling slightly to maintain. Maintain it she did, however, and continued.

"The day Nigel brought that medallion home and told me the story surrounding it, I thought it was a charming little item and felt that it might be an omen at least, if not an actual talisman. I don't really believe in that sort of thing you understand but, like most people I suppose, I'm not entirely impervious to the odd little superstition.

106

"The fact is, I hadn't told him that I was going to the clinic the next day to get the results of a pregnancy test. After ten years of trying and several disappointments, I didn't want to build his hopes up. I told him to put it in a drawer for safe keeping and, when I went out the next morning, I took it with me for luck. Silly I know, but there you are.

"Can you imagine the joy I felt when the results were positive? The elation was like nothing I had ever felt in my life; I was thrilled beyond anything I thought possible. I went to the supermarket and bought lots of special things for a celebratory dinner. I was skipping around like a silly schoolgirl and I was aching inside, wanting him to come home so that I could tell him the news.

"Ten minutes after I got back, the phone rang. It was your Mrs Evans. She thought I ought to know, she said, 'for my sake' etc, etc. She tried to sound sympathetic but I swear she was enjoying it. She might as well have come around in person and plunged a knife into my heart; that's what it felt like. The pain was physical as well as emotional. I broke down as soon as she rang off. I felt like an abandoned puppy that's been picked up by a prospective new owner and then dropped again.

"When Nigel came home I tore into him, as you can imagine. But I didn't tell him about the baby. Oh no! That was to be his punishment: keeping from him the thing he most wanted to hear. And, of course, I moved into the spare room. That was the second part of his punishment.

"After a couple of days I stopped crying and felt strangely calm, but I still hated him for what he'd done to me. So I developed this sort of detached attitude towards him. Started treating him like an imbecile; tried to make him feel small and insignificant. And I really enjoyed watching him deteriorate. I

107

revelled in it, sad as I am to say that now. And I continued to treat him like that until Saturday, two days ago.

"I suddenly had a change of heart. I don't know why, something suddenly came over me. I remembered how good things had once been between us and I decided that things could be like that again. I forgave him, I suppose. Odd that it should happen so suddenly. Perhaps that's how these things work, I don't know - I'm hardly an expert.

"Anyway, I decided to try and make it up between us, but it wasn't easy. His manner was defensive and suspicious. I felt upset and disappointed but I supposed it was understandable, given the way I'd been treating him for the past couple of weeks. And so, of course, I told him the wonderful news - about the baby. I expected him to be thrilled, overjoyed. I expected him to come back to me immediately. I had an image of him falling into my arms, weeping tears of joy. I wanted to hold him, tell him I forgave him, talk positively about the future. How very feminine and naïve of me!"

She stopped again and I saw undeniable signs that her composure was truly slipping.

"So what happened?" I asked after a decent pause.

She looked away and shook her head.

"I don't know," she said quietly.

Then she looked back at me. Her eyes were watering and her expression had changed to one of confusion. She took a lemon coloured tissue out of her bag and blew her nose discreetly. Slightly rejuvenated, she continued.

"Well, I do know, of course. But I don't understand it. He went – well – 'mad' is the only way I can put it. It was as though some horrible, dark dam had suddenly burst. His eyes became angry. No - more than angry: wild, like an

108

animal. I'd never seen that look in them before. They were so strange and fierce that I became frightened as well as disappointed.

"He rushed at me and grabbed my shoulders. He began shaking me violently and started shouting at me – strange things like 'why did you have to do it? Why with him you stupid bitch? Why him?' He kept on and on shaking me and shouting 'why him, why him?' over and over again. 'Why who?' I screamed back. I told him I didn't understand. I didn't know what he was talking about. *What* was I supposed to have done? *Who with*? I was completely bewildered.

"Then he started sobbing violently and sank down in a heap on the carpet. He kept punching the floor as hard as he could and saying 'Oh God no, not him. Why him?' through the sobs. I suppose I should have comforted him. Should I? I don't know. But I didn't; I just stood there. I hadn't a clue what was going on. He kept on sobbing and hitting the floor for ages while I began to think that I should call a doctor or an ambulance or something.

"Then he stopped and looked up at my stomach. His face was wild and twisted - and wet all over. It was coming from his eyes, his nose, his mouth. He looked disgusting. He raised himself to his knees and came towards me. I started backing away. And then he started prodding my stomach and shouting again, but more viciously this time. He'd stopped crying. More strange words came spitting out of his mouth. He started saying things like 'you won't get away with this Donald, you effing bastard. I'll see you in hell first. I'll destroy this effing demon of yours, so I will.'

"I'll never forget those last words. 'Demon?' What was that all about? And the expression 'so I will.' I'd never heard him say that before in all the years I'd known him. And who the hell's Donald?

"I decided it was time to dial 999 and started to walk towards the hall. He got up and said 'oh no you effing don't. You're not getting away that easily.' He ran into the kitchen and I heard the cutlery drawer fall to the floor with an almighty clatter. 'Oh God' I thought, 'he's gone for a knife.'

"I grabbed my bag and rushed out, meaning to get in the car and drive to a phone box. But he was coming through the front door by the time I got to the car. I knew I wouldn't have time to find the keys in the bag, unlock it, get in and lock it again; so I ran.

"Fortunately, a neighbour across the road was out in her garden and I shouted to her. She looked up and must have seen Nigel chasing me with a carving knife. Thankfully, she had the presence of mind to beckon me in and we slammed the door, just before Nigel started banging on it and stabbing it with the knife. I swear he would have killed me if he could have got at me. He was absolutely wild.

"My neighbour ran around to the back door, locked it and called the police. He went all around the house, shouting obscenities and kicking the doors. He even smashed a couple of windows but, thankfully, they were all small panes so he couldn't get in through any of them.

"The police got there very quickly – I suppose the whole street must have phoned them by then – and it wasn't long before I saw them taking him to one of those armoured vans they have. How they overcame him so quickly I don't know. Probably used CS spray I expect. He was still yelling when they took him down the path but I couldn't tell what it was. It sounded like 'Aaron go broke, or brought, or brat' - something like that. I assumed it was some garbled reference to the child. He shouted it several times before they bundled him into the van and drove him away.

"The police came and took a statement from me and said they'd be in touch. I've phoned them several times but all they'll tell me is that he's been taken to a secure mental hospital somewhere. They won't even let me see him until he's been thoroughly examined and 'evaluated' as they put it. So there's nothing I can do for now, except feel guilty. He must have been getting so near to the edge that the news about the baby made him flip."

She looked thoroughly drained when she finished the story and I felt genuinely shocked. I struggled to find something to say. The best I could manage was

"I shouldn't blame yourself too much. I'm sure it can't be as simple as that."

One corner of her mouth lifted slightly and she nodded briefly, as if to say "what the hell would you know?" I wanted to say something meaningful that might help her feel better, but all I had to offer was what Natalie and I had discovered in Ireland.

Nigel's reference to the name "Donald" appeared to add yet another twist to the story, but I felt unable to tell Sarah anything about that. I thought it would only load further heartache and confusion onto her. And that was if she believed a word of it, which I thought most unlikely. I was also reluctant to say anything that involved mentioning Natalie. Sarah might have stopped blaming me for her predicament, but Natalie was another matter altogether. Given the extent of my own interest in the affair, however, there was something I was curious about.

"What time did all this happen?" I asked.

"Around lunchtime," she replied. "Why? Is it important?"

Her expression indicated that she thought it a very odd question. No doubt it was, to someone who didn't know that it was about the same time that Natalie had been experiencing the disturbing events of 1916.

"No, of course not," I said hurriedly. "Just curious."

The statement didn't seem to help. I think Sarah must have regarded my apparently pointless question as indicating flippancy. She stood up and resumed her curt, organised manner.

"I take it I can leave it to you to inform your personnel office," she said abruptly. "I doubt he'll be back for a while. I imagine that things like this take a long time to recover from. And, of course, there might still be the question of a serious criminal charge."

I was aware that this was her polite way of pointing out the gravity of the situation. I assured her that I would take care of the necessary formalities and she began to walk towards the door. I was also aware that she would not take kindly to any more "flippant" questions, but there was something I was burning to know. I asked her, very apologetically, whether she still had the medallion. I said that it might help to solve a mystery. I had the impression that she thought my interest pecuniary, since she seemed to take a slightly peevish pleasure in replying with some harshness.

"No I haven't. When I came out of the clinic, I was so beside myself with joy that I actually gave the wretched thing some credence. There was a homeless woman sitting outside the building, so I gave it to her – said I hoped it would bring her luck. She was quite ungrateful; just put it into her pocket without even looking at it. She smiled at me and I gave her a ten pound note. She looked at *that* all right."

"I take it you never told Nigel that you'd given it away?"

112

"No, of course I didn't. He asked me where it was on one occasion but I was hardly in the mood to tell him anything, except that I'd put it where he wouldn't find it. I suppose the thing's valuable, is it?"

"It's not that," I said.

I felt that I had said too much to let her go without explaining my reason for asking such apparently irrelevant questions. I decided to take the plunge and said

"Can I show you something?"

I took the old photograph out of my desk drawer and placed it on the desk in front of her.

"Is this the woman you gave it to?" I asked, suddenly feeling slightly foolish.

She looked surprised.

"It does look very like her, yes. But I only saw her once. I could hardly be certain. Good gracious, doesn't he look like Nigel?"

She looked at me with a slight tilt of her head and a questioning frown on her brow.

"Where did you get this picture?" she asked. "Who are these people?"

"Sarah," I said hesitatingly, "do you believe in reincarnation?"

The tilt of her head remained, but her expression changed to one of derision.

"No, of course I don't. How ridiculous," she said sharply.

And so ended the possibility of an explanation.

"Just an odd coincidence then," I replied.

Sarah tutted and shook her head in annoyance. No doubt she had already got enough in her life that was inexplicable and deeply upsetting, without having to contend with what she undoubtedly saw as the bizarre line our conversation was now taking. She probably saw it as some juvenile attempt on my part to be unduly enigmatic. She walked out of my office without another word.

There had been no histrionics and no raised voices. Sarah had kept her emotions well under control throughout. And yet, when she'd gone, the sense of peace in the office was profound. As soon as she'd left the building, Natalie came in.

"Did you here any of that?" I asked her.

"Most of it," she said. "I was standing at the end of the banister until she was about to come out. Pretty weird eh? Seems like Nigel knows who he is now – or was. He obviously remembers Donal. And that phrase, Eireann go brath. It means 'Ireland for ever.' It was an old republican rallying call. It's another thing you hear in some old rebel songs. He must have thought he was being arrested by the RIC. Poor bloke."

"And it seems your great, great – however many it is – grandmother might have got her medallion back," I said. "I'm still having trouble taking all this in."

Natalie slumped into the vacant chair and we both sat in silence for some time, contemplating the latest twists in a story whose logic was both temptingly pragmatic and apparently preposterous at the same time. Logic, however, could not be denied and I was struck with a sense of wonder by the sublime irony of the latest revelations.

No curse, it seemed, had ever been effected. The medallion had been passed on in good time. And Nigel's fears about Sarah's pregnancy were both justified and baseless. She was obviously two or three months into her term before any of this had happened, and the child was clearly his own. Natalie broke the silence.

"You didn't tell her the story."

"No point. She wouldn't have believed it."

"No. Do you think there's anything we can do?"

"No."

There was more silence and then I heard male voices outside the window. I got up and looked out to see who it was.

"Paddy's outside," I said. "I wonder what he'll make of this picture."

I felt a small thrill of expectation as I took the photograph back out of the drawer. I hurried downstairs and out of the front door. There was a brief exchange of greetings and I noticed that Natalie was watching through my office window. I placed the picture on the wall beside him and pointed to the seated woman.

"Is that the woman who gave you the medallion?" I asked without ceremony or explanation.

He frowned and looked closely, then raised his eyebrows and leant back.

"Could be," he said uncertainly. "Aye, could well be, as far as I remember. But I couldn't be certain mate, now could I? I've drunk a lot of this stuff since then. Why? Who is she?"

"Look at the rest of the figures," I said.

He leant forward again. A puzzled look came over his face.

"Fuck me, David. That's me there, right enough. And isn't that your man – what's his name – the one who had the fling with the young floosie?"

"Nigel."

"Aye. And doesn't the young girl there look just like her? And this big ugly fella'; I'm sure I know him from somewhere, but I can't

115

place him. Where did you get this from?"

I told him the whole story, with just one diversion from the truth. I gave him Mary's version of Liam's actions, not Natalie's. I felt that it would cause her unnecessary embarrassment. Throughout the narrative, he divided his attention between me, the ground and his cider bottle. When I finished, he looked at me and smiled.

"You're not serious now, are you?"

I was disappointed. I felt my shoulders sag. Paddy obviously picked up on the fact.

"Come on now, mate," he said, making a brave attempt to hide his derision. "Good story and all that but, well..."

He shook his head dismissively and took another swig from his bottle. His friends had listened too and one of them sniggered.

"He didn't believe you, did he?" said Natalie when I went back to the office

"No. Don't suppose I should have expected him to really."

"We're on our own then, aren't we?" she concluded.

I didn't mind that. In fact, I suppose I preferred it that way. I asked her whether she still had thoughts on moving to Ireland.

"More than thoughts," she said positively. "I told you, I've decided. I wrote to Mary yesterday afternoon, asking if I could stay with her for a week or two while I look for a flat or something."

"What address did you send it to?"

"Mary Molloy, Buncrana, Road to Doorin Point, Donegal. I'm sure the local postie won't have trouble with that."

"No, don't suppose so. Have you got any money?"

"Oh yes, I've got a bit put by. I didn't spend it all on clubs and designer trainers, you know. And mum's quite keen on the idea, surprisingly enough. She says she'll help out if necessary. Dad thinks I'm nuts, but he'll come round. He always does."

"So when are you going?"

"Don't know yet. I'll see what Mary says. I'll probably wait until after Christmas I expect."

I felt despondent. I had only known Natalie – in any substantive sense that is – for a week, but already I felt that a bond had formed between us which was very rare. The prospect of her going way out west and breaking it seemed potentially very painful

"I'll miss you," I said.

"You don't have to. You could come with me," she replied.

There was that look again. It was warm and caring but, as usual, there was something more that I couldn't quite identify. I was conscious that my look in return was probably more like that of a scolded spaniel. I said nothing.

"Better get back to work," she said suddenly, as though she felt the need to disperse some powerful energy that hung in the air between us; an energy that seemed, to me at least, to be too enigmatic and restless even to be identified let alone resolved.

Chapter 9

For the next two months Natalie continued to take her lunch in my office, except on the odd day when she needed to go into town for something. It was on one such occasion that she had a copy of the old photograph made. She gave it to me and said that she intended to return the original to Mary. She didn't want one, she said; it made her feel uncomfortable, unsafe even.

We talked easily and incessantly on countless subjects, some that mattered and some that didn't. She told me that she had started to read about Buddhism, and said that it seemed to clarify and expand on a lot of what she had learned from me, as well as informing her own developing perceptions of life. It felt like a natural progression for her, she said, and she intended to pursue it further. It wasn't long before profound snippets of wisdoms started flowing back from her to add valuable insights to my own perceptions.

We talked about Nigel occasionally, though not as often as one might have expected. For, despite his pivotal role in the unfolding of recent events, I think there was a feeling on both our parts that he was now beyond us. In Natalie's case, I suspect that it would also be true to say that she wanted him and everything he stood for to be behind her.

Nevertheless, I felt it only proper to call Sarah a couple of times and check on his progress. She told me that the police had decided not to charge him, but his mental state showed little sign of improvement. She had been allowed to see him but he had refused to acknowledge her, spending the whole of her visit sitting upright in a chair with his head laid back and his eyes wandering aimlessly back and forth across the ceiling. The look in them was something she had never seen before, she said. The wildness that had burned in them on the day of his breakdown was gone. There was no anger, malice or bitterness. And yet she felt they were not dead eyes. There was something there, something touchingly sad and pitiable. The only expression she could find to describe their look was "profound resignation."

The doctors said that he was not always like that. Sometimes he became agitated and talked of curses, old enemies and a demon child sent to emasculate him. They regarded him as paranoid and used the phrase "seriously delusional." He had been sectioned for his own safety and that of others, especially his wife who, they believed, he would try to harm again if released into care at home.

She told me that her baby was expected some time in early March and that she was doing her best to live a normal life. Money was no problem since Nigel was still on sick leave and receiving full pay. She mentioned the photograph on one occasion and I sensed that she wanted to hear the full story. I felt nervous about how much I should tell her, but the moment passed as the subject changed and she never brought the matter up again.

During all the time I spent with Natalie there was one thing that we never talked about, even though I often considered it the most important thing of all. We never once went into the subject of our relationship. For my part, I can only say that it was because I felt confused. There is in me a degree of caution that prefers to avoid broaching contentious issues until I have developed some sort of a theorem on which to base my starting position. I had never been able to develop such a theorem in the case of my feelings for Natalie. The relative positions of the platonic and the romantic rose and fell in opposition to one another, rather like one of those beam engines that I had once thought so comparable with the hip movements of the pre-enlightened young woman.

I sometimes wondered why she had never brought the subject up. In my negative moments, I feared that it might be because I was simply not that important to her. At other times, however, it seemed that she was suppressing something. She was in the habit of visiting me at home at least twice a week, and occasionally I saw – or thought I saw – something in her eyes that spoke of an interest beyond mere friendship.

Throughout it all I was conscious of the fact there was a substantial age gap between us. Even had there been a mutual romantic attraction, such a difference would probably have discouraged us from pursuing it. And she only mentioned the prospect of my accompanying her to Ireland on one further occasion.

It was after I'd made some comment about being unsettled and needing a change of scene. The remark was made idly, but Natalie picked up on it with some enthusiasm.

"Donegal would be a change of scene," she said.

"Bit of a big step," I replied.

It sounded pathetic, even to me, but I knew that my excessive caution was due more to the undefined nature of our relationship than to any inherent reluctance to make major moves. I hoped that she would sense as much, but she continued the interrogation briefly.

"Why?" she asked, apparently a little exasperated. "It's not as though you've got close family here, or any great social life."

Although I felt pressured, I was buoyed by such an obvious indication that she wanted me to stay close. For a second or two the urge to plunge into unknown

120

territory gripped me; but then the confusion of uncertainty reasserted its hold and I continued with my feeble excuses.

"I know, but I've got a well paid job here, haven't I? And then I'd have to sell the house. That can take ages sometimes. And, well, I suppose I know this area. I'm comfortable here."

She looked unconvinced and disappointed.

"Fair enough," she said with little conviction.

By then she had told me that her great grandmother had written back to say that she would be delighted to act as host for as long as it took Natalie to find accommodation. She would be thrilled, she said, to have a member of her family so close again. I felt pleased that Natalie would be living in a house, albeit temporarily, that she would inevitably associate with me. It helped to salve the dismay I felt at the prospect of losing her.

The approach of the Christmas holiday only served to heighten my sense of apprehension. Going to the office in the morning had become an act of pleasure since our return from Ireland, and I had no appetite for what I saw as the approaching emptiness of the ten day break. She would come to see me at home, of course, but it wouldn't be the same as our habitual, daily routine of working and having lunch together.

Christmas Day fell on a Saturday that year and she said that she felt obliged to spend it with her parents, especially since it would probably be the last for some time. She offered to spend the whole of Boxing Day with me and I accepted graciously, even though I felt a sting of irritation at the idea that I was being relegated to second place. My disappointment must have showed. She smiled and said

"OK. Don't suppose the folks will mind if I spend a few hours out, once we've finished with the presents. They're planning to go to some posh hotel for Christmas dinner anyway – give mum a break from the cooking. You can have the trouble of feeding me if you like."

I smiled a guilty but grateful smile back.

She came around at eleven. We each handed the other a small package, wrapped in Christmas paper. They looked remarkably similar. Indeed they should, for they were both items of jewellery to be worn "in memoriam," Natalie's gift to me was a silver neck chain. It had a small claddagh, symbol of eternal friendship, hanging on it. Mine to her was a bracelet with inset shamrock links, to bring her good luck.

We talked of sundry matters as usual, had lunch and then watched a film on the TV. When it was over I went to fetch coffee and mince pies. I returned to find that she had turned off one of the table lamps in the living room and was standing by the window, watching a light snow falling in the gathering gloom of twilight. I put the tray on the coffee table and went to join her.

There was a film of virgin whiteness covering the lawns, road and rooftops. It was that quiet, lethargic part of Christmas Day when people are mostly either resting their over-taxed digestive systems or watching the festive special of some popular programme on the television. There were neither people nor cars to disturb the surreal serenity of the street. In the window of a house opposite, an illuminated, red and green Father Christmas flashed on and off. And, if that were not enough, a majestic full moon was already showing its splendid face in the darkening sky above the white roofs. I think we both felt the same profound sense of a rare peace settling on a troubled world.

"Perfect, isn't it," she said. "Just how Christmas should be, especially a last one."

The poignancy of the moment gripped me. Outside the house, the perfection of the new-laid snow, the peace of the half-lit, deserted street, and the vibrant colours of the Christmas icon shining like a beacon in the gloom, seemed to represent a message telling me that all was right with the world. Inside the house, and inside my heart, was the knowledge that something very precious was about to be taken out of my life. The contrast was profound. It seemed irreconcilable, and I struggled to know how I should respond or what meaning I should infer from it. I was glad that my instinct was to feel privileged. If this was to be the last Christmas we would spend together, how right that it should favour us with such exquisite perfection. She wrapped her arm gently around mine and said

"January 8th, that's when I'm going."

The news, though not unexpected, shocked me; and the sudden ache that started in the pit of my stomach soon rose to my throat where it settled as a painful knot. I remained phlegmatic.

"Right," I said. "Let's have this coffee."

I managed to stay rational and objective and asked her about the practical arrangements. What time was the sailing, when would she give in her notice, how much stuff would she be taking with her, that sort of thing. I wasn't really interested in any of it, of course, but it seemed like the right thing to ask; partly because it was polite, but mostly because concentration on the trivial was an effective way of subduing the rising sense of panic at my impending loss.

The sailing was in the morning, she said. She would give in her notice when the office reopened and wouldn't worry that it was less than her contract required. She

123

was sure that all she needed would fit in the car. There was no mention of my going with her.

She visited me several times more over the course of the following week, but there was no more talk of her imminent emigration. Not, that is, until New Year's Eve which she spent lazily reclining on my sofa. I suppose it was inevitable that it should come up that night, when it is customary for thoughts to be dominated by reflections on the year past and aspirations for the one ahead.

"Big one this year, eh," she said after Big Ben had performed its annual duty, the post-midnight fireworks had finished and I'd turned off the TV.

The words broke an uneasy silence that had hung over us for some time. I didn't really want to talk about the matter but felt obliged to remain polite.

"You all packed then?"

"Mostly," she said with no show of enthusiasm. "Haven't got that much to take really. Some clothes, a few books, bits and pieces. I'll need to find somewhere furnished when I get over there."

For a moment I saw that look again. It was even more intense than usual and I thought she was about to say something further. Then it faded and she declared that it was about time she went home.

The return to work on 4th January was not a joyful affair. I was too conscious that this was the final stage of a descent into something I didn't want to face. Four more days of having Natalie close by and then it would be all over. I think she felt it too. Our conversations were less free than usual and it was clear that we had both erected defensive walls that were blocking our usual, easy communication.

On the Friday she divided her time between clearing her desk and sitting in my office talking pointless trivia. I was in no mood for working either. Before she went home, she said that she would come around later that night to say goodbye. She would have to leave very early the next morning, she said, as the sailing was at eight fifty five.

Strange as it may sound, the details of the final hour we spent together in my house were too banal to recount. Suffice it to say that the atmosphere was tense and our respective manners stolidly matter-of-fact. In my case, it was the standard defensive contrivance to enable me to get through the event without making a fool of myself. I hoped it was the same for Natalie. More than that, I indulged my ego by assuming that her apparent denial of the emotional gravity of the occasion was necessary to prevent her giving in and changing her mind. It wasn't until our final few moments together that something of what was truly in her heart came rushing forth. We exchanged a stronger-than-usual hug on the pavement beside her car.

"Don't let me go Dave," she said suddenly, with an earnestness bordering on desperation pouring from her eyes.

For a moment I thought she was asking me to say something that she wanted to hear, something to give her a reason not to go. But then she continued.

"Emotionally, I mean. Not yet anyway - not until I've written to you and explained something I haven't dared tell you to your face."

She paused for a moment and looked at the ground. I took the opportunity to jump in.

"Dared tell me? What haven't you dared tell me? What's happened?"

This was more than just intriguing. I felt frightened. She shook her head and looked up into my eyes again.

"Nothing's *happened* as such," she continued. "It's to do with something *I* know but you don't. But I need to put some space between us before I tell you. That's a bit of the reason why I decided to go away, apart from the fact that I really do want to go back to my roots.

"I'll write to you, I promise - soon. I thought of writing a letter and posting it today so you'd get it on Monday. But I just couldn't seem to find the right opportunity this week, what with mum fussing around and everything. And I had trouble finding the right words as well. It's been going over and over in my head all week. I know what I need to say, it's just a matter of finding the right way of saying it. I'm not quite as good at that as you are. I'm sure it'll be clearer once I'm over there and smelling the salt coming off Donegal Bay. So please be patient, OK?"

She had her hands on my upper arms all the time she was talking. She kept moving them slowly up and down, as though she were trying to comfort me and excise her own frustrations at the same time.

"You look frightened," she said fondly. "Don't be. It's me who's got the reason to be frightened. And I am, believe me. I know I've never said this before, and I know you might find it hard to believe, but I really do love you, you know. And now I'm going."

She climbed into her car while I stood on the pavement feeling dazed, empty, wretched and elated, all at the same time. I heard the engine start, smelt the exhaust fumes as her car pulled away from the kerb, and watched her brake lights come on as she prepared to turn the first corner. I lifted my arm in a half-hearted wave. I couldn't tell whether she waved back; I could only hope that she had. And then she passed out of sight behind a row of cold, dark houses. The sound of her little red Citroen soon faded to nothing.

For the sake of my own pride, I should prefer not to describe the state I was in for at least half an hour after I went back into the house. And I think I only recovered as quickly as I did because I had the tantalizing prospect of the mysterious letter to hang onto.

Chapter 10

Work would never be the same again. That much was obvious long before I dragged myself to the office on Monday morning. I hadn't wanted to get up, shave or do any of the things that constituted the normal prelude to a working day. Breakfast had been a savourless chore, taken only out of a sense of duty to shape up and carry on.

It was a fine, mild morning for early January, but I was hardly in the mood to appreciate it. As I approached the building I saw Paddy, cigarette in one hand and cider bottle in the other as usual, standing on the porch and looking full of the joys of the still-distant spring.

"Morning David," he said perkily. "Nice day, eh?"

"Yes, I suppose it is," was the best I could manage in reply.

"You look a bit down mate."

"Do I? Never mind. We all have problems, don't we?"

He ignored the question and continued brightly.

"I hear the wee minx has left."

"Paddy, she isn't a minx, you know. She's actually a very decent and intelligent young woman."

"Aye, well, if you say so mate. You ought to know, eh?"

He didn't actually wink, or go so far as to nudge my arm, but his expression made it plainly obvious that my closeness to Natalie had not gone unnoticed. It was also inevitable, I suppose, that it had probably been misconstrued.

"I haven't seen your friend Nigel for a long time either," he continued. "Yer woman with the sour face tells me he's got some trouble

- up here, like." He tapped the side of his head.

Mrs Evans was usually the least inclined of all of us to exchange chit-chat with the drinkers. She regarded all alcoholic beverages as the Devil's brew, and those who fell under its spell as being clearly beyond the pale and having no hope of redemption. But I suppose the undoubted delight she could take in proclaiming the downfall of a sinner helped her to overcome her reticence in this instance, no matter what the standard of the congregation.

"Yes, he has," I said curtly. "Something like that."

"Well, I told you now, didn't I? He should have got rid of that medal thing, so he should."

I wondered why Paddy, along with most other people no doubt, could be so certain of the efficacy of talismans and the real threat of curses, whilst being unable even to contemplate the possibility of reincarnation. I supposed that superstition belonged to the exclusive perception of current, physical existence. Looking beyond it to the concept of a cycle of life, death and rebirth was a little further removed.

But I couldn't be bothered to bring the matter up for discussion. Neither could I be bothered to tell him that the medallion *had* been passed on, and that the curse was nothing more than a red herring. I went into the building and made straight for the foot of the stairs. As I did so, I heard Mrs Evans coming out of the staff dining room. She was talking to somebody and the first words I heard were

"So perhaps he'll get some work done, now the strumpet has taken herself off to the bogs where they still worship the pope."

She was talking to a young woman who I assumed was an accounts trainee on secondment. For all her faults, Mrs Evans was very good at her job and trainees were occasionally sent to her for experience. I have to be honest and admit that I enjoyed the look on her face when she realised that I'd overheard her peevish remark. Her frosty features burned for once with the red hot fire of embarrassment. I returned her startled gaze with a contemptuous look of my own and proceeded on my way.

I went into Natalie's office and looked wistfully at the clear desk and the chair pushed neatly underneath it. I sat in it for a while, hoping it would help me to feel closer to her. I suppose it did in a way, but it was no substitute for her physical presence and I soon got up and went to my own room. I was just forcing myself unwillingly into the humdrum business of the day when the phone rang.

It was the woman from personnel, the one who had refused to give me Nigel's number all those eons ago. She said that she was sending someone over as a replacement for Natalie. The notion was preposterous; no-one could replace Natalie. His name was Ben, she said. He was a promising young man who had just completed a course in word processing. She asked me to show him where everything was and to keep an eye on him. I gave her the most diligent undertaking I could muster in the circumstances.

Then we talked briefly about Nigel. She trotted out all the predictable sentiments: how terrible his illness must be for him, what a shame it was for his wife, how it couldn't have come at a worse time – what with the baby being due in a couple of months - and so on. I felt dishonest, having to pretend that I knew little more than she did about the circumstances surrounding Nigel's spectacular fall from normality. I tried to keep my replies to words of one syllable and hoped that my carefully modulated vocal tones would make up for my lack of verbal response. I doubted that she really cared all that much anyway. Few of us respond to the suffering of others as deeply as we like to pretend we do.

Ben arrived half an hour later. I saw him walking shabbily across from the car park as I was about to get a cup of coffee. He had his mobile phone in one hand and was tapping on the keys with his thumb. The other hand was engaged in the process of idly scratching his groin. He didn't look terribly promising to me. And my pessimism seemed all the more justified when I opened the front door to him.

At close quarters he looked pale and listless. His hair was heavily gelled and he was wearing an ill-fitting suit of some slightly shiny fabric. The colour of his shirt was at odds with the colour of his suit, and the tie that hung limply off-centre from a badly formed knot was at odds with just about everything known to man or nature. I imagined that he had previously worked, unsuccessfully probably, as a commission-only double glazing salesman.

I was in no mood to feel kindly towards Ben, but I reminded myself of the impressions I had formed about Natalie until she had revealed her true colours. I thought I was probably being presumptuous at least, if not actually vindictive. Perhaps Ben had hidden qualities too. Perhaps they would rise to the fore when the time was right, as Natalie's had. I doubted it somehow. It seemed to me that nature endows young women with so much more openness to the potential for growth, once the possibility is presented to them. And they seem to be naturally endowed with a lot more of that inner vitality necessary to achieve it. I had often wondered whether it was due to some innate psychological or spiritual difference between the sexes, or whether it was all down to social conditioning.

At any rate, I decided that such rapidly formed impressions of Ben were unbecoming, and

131

probably unfair. I showed him where everything was, introduced him to the rest of the staff and explained the office routines. Most of his responses were, I still have to say, largely or completely unintelligible; but he seemed happy enough to start work. I went back to my office and tried not to think of him sitting in Natalie's chair.

I didn't stop thinking about Natalie though. Her speech to me on Saturday night ran over and over in my head. I wondered how long it would be before the letter arrived, and I wondered what it would say. I imagined it saying all sorts of things, some of them good and some of them bad. The twin sensations of heady optimism and abject panic fought each other constantly and I found it difficult to concentrate on the mundane matter of my workload.

I judged the tone of Natalie's speech to have been ominous, but realised that my judgement was probably being clouded by a heavy veil of insecurity. And I knew that my anxiety would not fade as the days passed. I wondered what she would be doing at that moment, and hoped that she would be sitting somewhere, writing the letter. That much was certain. I was desperate to hear what she so desperately needed to say. And I wanted to hear it now.

Thus began the routine of my going anxiously to the letterbox first thing every morning, and of my becoming increasingly frustrated every time there was no envelope with an Irish postmark. After two weeks I began to suspect that the postal service must be at fault, or even the postman.

I knew that some people disliked the Irish. The IRA atrocities of the 1970s had instilled in many people a narrow-minded belief that the whole Irish nation was somehow complicit in those terrible, bloody acts, and had developed an almost pathological mistrust of them. I had known a few such people myself

132

and I wondered if our cheerful postman was secretly so inclined. I imagined him taking all the mail with Irish stamps attached back home with him and burning them on a ceremonial bonfire.

For most of the day, such thoughts seemed ridiculous. But they rose up again every time I went downstairs in the morning to find nothing but bills and junk mail. My frustration reached such a pitch that I even stopped taking breakfast, and I became known in the office as someone who was to be avoided, if at all possible, for at least the first hour of the day.

And the office provided nothing in the way of help for my state of mind. The work was generally dull and predictable, and I had never made any friends among the small staff who worked there. My initial impressions of Ben were proving accurate and he was supremely ignorable. Mrs Evans was becoming more objectionable than ever, and the rest fell somewhere between the two. I realised that my life had been lacking any real content or purpose even before the dramatic events of the last few months, but I'd never really noticed the fact until now. The loss of Natalie brought it home to me very firmly.

I became increasingly tense and inwardly dismissive of everything except a persistent ache born of the question that was constantly gripping me: why had Natalie not written yet? At times I convinced myself that I should hate her for putting me through all this. It didn't last, of course; the desperate need to make contact with her increased as each day went by. What did last, far longer than they were entitled to, were the hours that made up the working day. They seemed to go on interminably.

And then, on the last day of January, I was shaken out of my morbid self-obsession when I had a phone call from personnel. They had been notified by Sarah that

133

Nigel had died. They knew little of the circumstances but thought I should let the rest of the office know. They didn't have a date for the funeral yet as there were certain formalities still to be concluded.

I felt that I should ring Sarah. I thought it only proper since I was genuinely saddened and wanted to offer my condolences. I was also troubled by a brief revival of my old sense of guilt and I was curious to know the details. It seemed to me that the drama was still unfolding, and that the circumstances of Nigel's death might shed one more ray of light on the plot. It might even presage the lowering of the final curtain.

But I was struck by the fact that she had gone straight to personnel this time, and not communicated with them through me as she had done before. I wondered whether she preferred not to talk to me. I decided to call her anyway, later that night, if only for the sake of propriety. In the event, she called me shortly after I arrived home.

She told me that a couple of weeks after the police had decided not to press charges, Nigel had been transferred to a less secure mental hospital closer to home. He had even started to make progress. He remained paranoid and delusional, she said, but the state of extreme apathy and detachment into which he had fallen had begun to lift. And the occasional bouts of agitated raving had become less frequent and less severe. As a result, he had been given a little more freedom to move about and had taken the opportunity with some semblance of enthusiasm.

And then, two days before on the Saturday morning, he had been in the common room with a group of other patients which included a young girl of around twelve or thirteen. The staff had been alerted to a commotion going on and had seen Nigel taking "an unhealthy physical interest", as she put it, in the young girl. When they moved quickly to separate him from her, he had taken flight, rushed out of the room and fallen down a short flight of stone steps that led to the entrance hall. Despite having gone down only four steps, his neck had been broken and he was dead. A routine post mortem had been held and the funeral was arranged for Friday. She went on to say that the circumstances might require that a formal enquiry be carried out and, if so, she hoped that she would not have to be involved.

As she recounted the events, Sarah remained as lucid and emotionally organised as she had been when she came to see me in the office. I wondered, even while she was speaking, whether such commendable control was simply a function of her cool and formal nature, or whether she had effectively given up on Nigel and was vesting her hopes for the future entirely in her unborn child. Whatever the reason, there was little I could do except offer my sympathy and tell her that I would circulate details of the funeral around the office.

Before she rang off, however, she remarked in a tone of uncharacteristic uncertainty that Nigel's illness had probably reawakened his old weakness for attractive young women, but how he could be interested in a girl as young as that she found difficult to understand. She could only suppose that it must have been a bizarre consequence of his unbalanced state of mind.

I thought of little else while I was making and eating my dinner. Briefly, I imagined the event through the eyes of the young girl and it horrified me to realise that she would have seen the same face as Brigit had seen all those years ago. I was glad that she had been spared the same ordeal. The thought caused me to make a connection with Natalie, and I wondered what she had been doing while all this was going on. I wondered whether she had been looking at the photograph again, and whether some energy might have been generated that had nudged the final move in the game that fate had been playing so expertly with us during the last three months.

I felt some sympathy for Sarah of course, but it struck me that Nigel's demise could be said to be fitting and well timed. The echoes of his old crimes had come back to him in full measure and had now been assuaged. The cycle of cause and effect had completed its round and the purpose of his current incarnation been fully served. I was reminded of Shakespeare's succinct insight into the nature of life and death.

We are such stuff as dreams are made on; and our little life is rounded with a sleep.

It seemed oddly fitting that I didn't get Natalie's letter until a couple of hours after Nigel's funeral.

The event had been a gloomy affair in the middle of a gloomy February afternoon. Sarah had looked less elegant than when I had last seen her, mainly because of her burgeoning shape and the unflattering nature of her maternity apparel. A few stilted pleasantries had been exchanged, and there were the usual expressions of contrived plaudits for the deceased. And, predictably I suppose, the irrepressible Mrs Evans had presumed to give Sarah the benefit of her certainties regarding the love of Jesus, the hope of forgiveness, and the prospect of life everlasting. She had also been the only one of the office staff to invite herself back to the house for tea. When I heard that, I had felt even more sympathy for Sarah. The rest of us had been more diplomatic. We had gone back to the office after the service, cleared up the loose ends, and then closed the building earlier than usual.

When I arrived home I found a thick envelope lying on the mat. The postman must have been late that morning. I felt a slight thumping in my chest as I picked it up and turned it over. The stamp was Irish and the handwriting unquestionably Natalie's.

Strangely, or perhaps it wasn't so strange really, I didn't rip it open immediately. I was nervous and carried it through to the kitchen while I got used to having it in my hands at last. I took a knife out of the drawer and slid it carefully under the fold at the top. The rasping sound as I sliced the paper seemed ominous – so ominous, in fact, that I put it down again and made a cup of tea first. Then I took it through to the living room, sat in my armchair where the light of the table lamp was brightest, and prepared myself finally to read what Natalie had to say. And this was it.

Dearest Dave

Here it is at last. Sorry it's taken me so long to write but this is the third version. The other two got chucked. I've also been finding it more difficult than I thought, getting a job and finding somewhere to live. Donegal's not a very big place, as you know. Fortunately I've managed to kill two birds with one stone. I've got a job in one of the tea shops in the town, not far from the place we went to. There's a small flat on the top floor and the owner says I can use it for a pretty small rent. The pay's poor but at least I won't have to spend money on travelling so I'll get by OK. It'll tide me over for the time being anyway. I'm moving into the flat on Saturday (the 5th) and start work on Monday morning.

Mary's been really good to me and I've had a lovely time staying with her. I'm glad to be getting out from under her feet though, even if she doesn't seem to see it that way. She said I could stay there as long as I liked and she made me promise to visit her at least once a week. She really is a sweetie. I gave her the original of that photograph back. It made me feel uneasy, carrying it around. I felt it most last Saturday morning when I saw it lying on the old dresser that stands on the wall opposite the range. I looked at it and suddenly saw Liam's face coming towards me again. It made me feel sick and frightened, like he was reaching out to get me. I take it Nigel's still in the asylum is he? I'd hate to think he was following me over here. (Not very likely, I know. Now who's getting paranoid?)

You'll like this bit. I've discovered that there's some sort of Buddhist centre in Derry, so I'm going to go and check it out. It's not too far to drive and you don't have to go through checkpoints any more. If I like it I might make it a regular trip, say twice a month or something. People around here go to Derry for the sort of shopping they can't get in Donegal, so I can combine the two - if I've got any money that is!

Right, that's the easy stuff dealt with. Now we come to the difficult bit. Well, two bits actually, only they're not exactly 'bits.' These are what I had so much trouble with at the first two attempts, but I'm determined to get them right this time.

Firstly – prepare yourself for a shock – I'm pregnant. I had pretty strong suspicions before I came over here but now it's confirmed. It has to be Nigel's, of course. It couldn't be anybody else's. I wasn't on the pill you see. Like I said, I wasn't the good time girl everybody thought I was!

I can't say I'm very happy about it being his, as you'd expect. But what can I do? The nurse suggested I go back to England and get an abortion. It's not so easy over *here. I didn't even consider it. I remembered what Mary said about taking a life. That's what she is, isn't she – a human life with a potential future. (I know it's going to be a girl – family tradition!) How could I even consider denying her that future? I hate all that modern stuff about freedom of choice. How can pro-choice be more important than pro-life? Can't be right, can it, however much it fits in with modern culture. I hope you agree, as I'm sure you probably do. You're not much of a fan of modern culture yourself, are you?*

I told Mary the news yesterday. She gave me a smug, 'I told you so' sort of look and said "Well it had to come soon, didn't it dear. You'll be twenty next week." I don't think there's much she doesn't know, and I'm sure she'll be very supportive. I'll have to write to the parents next and tell them. Mum will be OK but I'm not so sure about dad. It takes him six months to get used to having a new toothbrush, let alone something as big as this!

I'm going to call her Aisling Mary. In case you don't know, Aisling is pronounced 'Ashling' and means 'dream' or 'vision.' It seems right for her because I'm convinced that she's going to be something bright and beautiful growing out of a vision of something dark and disgusting – like those wild flowers that grew out of the bomb sites during the war. And I just had to add Mary didn't I? Couldn't not do. So, that's the first bombshell dropped. Hope you're still with me.

The next bit is the most difficult of all. It's what was bothering me before I left and what I didn't want to tell you till there was space between us. I wanted you to be able to think about it and get your feelings clear without me hanging around and putting pressure on you.

It concerns what we are to each other – our relationship. Ever since that first week when I spent

140

all that time in your office, I've been feeling closer and closer to you. But I've been confused about what sort of closeness it should be. I had the impression lots of times that it was bothering you too. I didn't know whether you knew what you wanted but didn't like to say, or whether you were as confused as me. I was so grateful that you never brought it up and put pressure on me – thanks for that.

At first it was mainly the age gap that was making me uncertain. Not that I objected, I just wasn't sure whether it could work. By the time we went to Ireland together, I'd decided that age meant nothing and was all ready to pluck up the courage and talk to you about it – see how you felt. What confused everything again was that photograph and the visions I had about Liam/Nigel. You remember me saying that I didn't know how to feel about Nigel now? How I knew he was a different person in this life and wasn't Liam anymore, but I still couldn't forget who he used to be? Well (God, here goes!), I'm afraid that the same thing applies to you.

There's one thing I left out when I was telling you about Liam coming into my bedroom that day. All through that horrible ordeal, I kept looking at a small photograph in a frame beside my bed. It was a picture of my parents, taken before I was born I suppose – mum looked very young. In my terror and confusion, I kept wishing that they would come and rescue me somehow, even though I knew my dad was dead. And guess who my dad looked exactly like! That's what I've known all these months – that you were my dad who died before I was really old enough to know him.

So now can you understand why I always kept some physical distance between us? Why I never gave myself to you, body and soul, like I wanted to? Sometimes I think of you as a totally different person. The first thing I thought when I learned about the pregnancy was how much I wanted it to be yours, not Nigel's. But I can't get that picture out of my head. I can't totally get rid of the knowledge of who you used to be, even if it was in a previous life. I know that we're both living in different bodies now. Physically, at least, we're not the same people. So does that make it all right? I still don't know.

And there's another factor involved too. There's something about this Buddhist stuff that makes me want to be independent. I don't feel the same need for the man-woman thing that I used to. I think I could be quite content being a free spirit – well, as free as you can be when you're bringing up a child. But, and I know this is going to sound selfish, I still want you near me – near us. When I told you I loved you, I really meant it. I feel a deep closeness to you that I've never felt for anybody else. And I can't think of a better influence on Aisling while she's growing up. I'd even be prepared to move back to England if I knew you could accept me on the basis of what I've just told you. As much as I love Mary, and as much as I feel at home here, there's been a constant ache inside me these last few weeks. I've missed you like hell!

I have to accept that you might not be happy with all this. Please think about it and let me know – either way. I'd rather have a 'no' than nothing. I'm not sure what the exact address of the flat is yet. I'll find out when I move in and send you a postcard on Monday.

Write back as soon as you can – please.

All my love,

Natalie.

Bombshells? They were certainly that and, true to the metaphor, they left me reeling

142

and confused. I read the letter several times, put it aside and then read it again. I went off and did some household chores; I made another coffee and idly read a few news items on Teletext; I made my dinner and ate it without really tasting a mouthful. Gradually, the fog cleared. A warm and welcome lightness of spirit started to dawn on me, and the numbness that I had been feeling was replaced with a tingle of vibrant energy.

For a start, Natalie's revelation about my identity in her previous life cleared up the one mystery that remained. I had occasionally wondered whether I had played any part in the old story. Seeing no obvious parallel between myself and any of the identifiable characters, I had assumed that my position in the present train of events had been merely that of catalyst, some sort of go-between necessary for the chain of circumstances to be effectively linked. Now that the truth had been revealed, it clearly altered the situation and possibly explained why I had been so reluctant to declare one aspect of my feelings to Natalie. But it also placed all relevant factors out in the open, and that would enable us to proceed with honesty and a clear conscience.

My future suddenly seemed more positive. The details were a mystery, certainly, but so what? I felt a sense of purpose and belonging at last. Natalie wanted to be close to me and I wanted to be close to her. Since both facts allowed no room for doubt any longer, there was only one option open to me; and it was an option that I was very happy about exercising. Whatever road our relationship took would be all right with me. There was clearly a bond of such depth and persistence between us that denial would have stood contrary to both logic and the natural order of the universe.

And then I began to see pictures in my mind. They were exquisite pictures plucked at random from the seemingly infinite reel of a rosy future, the sort of pictures whose only value is in their own, self-contained reality. Rarely do they constitute anything more than a poor shadow of their ultimate expression which always falls short of, exceeds, or alters the original. But see them we do. And so we should; because it is only through our capacity to meditate, dream and visualise that we can create our own reality, uncorrupted by external forces.

I saw an image of us sitting together on the promontory beyond the old abbey, watching in silence as the westering sun set Donegal Bay ablaze. I saw us tramping through the misty mountains, moistening our hands in the May morning dew. I saw us standing on some cliff or headland out on the western fringes, braced against the gale with watering eyes, and marvelling at the power of the wide Atlantic.

But, most of all, I saw us walking down that quiet lane that led to Doorin Point. I saw the splendour of those raggedy gorse bushes, replete with the golden mantle of early summer. I thought of the sheep that had watched us pass by once before, and whose lambs would still be frolicking like playful children, precursors of the new life that would shortly shine forth out of Natalie's dark past. And I imagined that, at such mystical and meaningful moments, we might descend into playful and meaningless conversations.

"So," I would ask as the seabirds wheeled above us and cried their plaintive, primeval call, "who do you think Mrs Evans was in a previous life?"

"Lucretia Borgia," Natalie would answer immediately, her stare remaining fixed on the setting sun.

"No, not bright enough. How about Matthew Hopkins?"

"Who's he?"

"The Witchfinder General. A man who made a good living burning innocent people and telling everybody it was God's will."

"Oh," would be her half-hearted reply after another pause. "No, I know what *she* was."

"What's that?"

"A can-can dancer in the Follies Berger."

I would snigger and repeat her statement incredulously. I would question where on earth she got that one from, but her reply would be as rational as ever.

"Well, she's such a sour-faced, hypocritical, sanctimonious old bigot that I reckon she's making up for a decadent past in a previous life. I wonder if she realises just how bad an advert for Christianity she really is."

"Mm, suppose so," I would reply earnestly. "It does make a certain sense. But did you know what 'sanctimonious' meant before you met me?"

She would give me one of those withering, dismissive, delightful looks again, and my reason for being there would be well and truly endorsed.

At that point the mental wandering stopped and returned to the mundane realities of the present moment. I went off to wash the dishes. Even then, however, the image of Mrs Evans cavorting suggestively in frilly knickers and fishnet stockings, held up with embroidered garters, swam repeatedly into my mind. I saw a crowd of dishevelled, lascivious Frenchmen with Clouseau accents, shouting their approbation with great enthusiasm, and I allowed myself the indulgence of a childish chuckle.

Whether any of my fondly imagined scenarios would ever come to pass and, if they did, how they would compare with the originals, there was no way of predicting. But then, finding out is all part of the magic and mystery of life. There was, however, one serious issue that I would have to bring to Natalie's attention. I would have to tell her about Nigel's death.

I felt apprehensive about that. It seemed inevitable that she would suffer a fresh wave of guilt, and not without some justification. There could be no denying that, had she not gone out with him that lunchtime, he would probably still be alive, working happily away in the quiet little building in the park and looking forward to the birth of his first child.

But then, it was I who had given him the medallion in the first place - an action that, at one time at least, had seemed to trigger the course of subsequent events. I could have no way of knowing whether it really had generated the "luck" that had been promised, or whether that had been a red herring too. And I could take solace from the fact that I had been merely the third cog in the chain.

That realisation raised another spectre, however. I began to see the four of us – the woman in the Belfast playground, Paddy, Natalie and me – as conspirators in a dark plot to send Nigel to a painful and ignominious end. No, I thought, that surely couldn't be right. Whoever the mysterious woman was, I could be sure that the rest of us had been entirely ignorant of any "game" being played and had performed our roles, if such they were, without any semblance of malice.

I hoped and trusted that I could convince Natalie to take the same philosophical view of the situation. I hoped that she would understand that the workings of something far beyond our capacity even fully to understand, let

146

alone control, had been guiding the course of events. And I hoped that she would see the rightness of it all. If her visions or memories of Liam's terrible, twin betrayals had been correct - as I was sure they had been - then justice had been done and the universe was unfolding as it should. For my own part, I let the matter rest at that.

I spent the next week making arrangements. The house was put on the market, I made an appointment to have my furniture taken into store, and I sorted out my finances. It seemed a good idea to have my savings transferred to my current account for the time being. I would have to spend some money soon and I wanted it to be easily accessible. And I gave two weeks notice to personnel. They weren't happy – my conditions stipulated a month – but they accepted it grudgingly.

On the Friday, Natalie's postcard arrived. I posted one back on my way to work. It simply said "How do you feel about an overnight guest? Can I sleep on your sofa? Clothes line not acceptable. Be with you soon."

As I walked across the verge from the car park that morning, I noticed that the spaces between the trees were awash with clumps of snowdrops. They looked marvellously vibrant, as snowdrops always do at that time of year, their green leaves and white flowers standing proud among the brown earth, dark tree trunks and leafless branches. I had always seen them as Mother Nature's first whispering of optimism, telling us that the cycle of the seasons has turned upwards and the cold, dark days of winter are on the wane.

That day, the sight of them held a second, more profound meaning. I saw them as symbolising the new life growing in Natalie, the resurgence of my own prospects, and the ending of a dark story that had spanned six generations. More than that even, they seemed to represent a personal message from the

Universe, telling me that it really was unerringly on course and that my prospective move was entirely right.

Paddy was sitting on the wall as I approached the building. I hadn't seen him since a few days before Nigel's funeral.

"You're looking better today, mate," he said. "Won the lottery or something?"

I told him that I was moving to his neck of the woods. Well, near enough anyway. He told me that he had family in Donegal.

"Aye. Belfast, Derry and Donegal; that's where my family are."

I wasn't surprised. I doubted that any coincidental connection would ever surprise me again. And then he asked, with a note of suspicion in his voice.

"You're not following the wee girl over there, are you?"

I smiled as he looked searchingly into my face. What he saw must have given him the clue he was seeking, for his tone changed to one of reprimand.

"You could be heading for trouble there, David. She's a bit young for you, you know. She could be your daughter, so she could."

Any reply on my part would have been redundant. I walked away from him up the path, shaking my head at the small but sublime irony contained within his observation. And, for the first time in several months, I laughed out loud.

www.ingramcontent.com/pod-product-compliance
Lightning Source LLC
Chambersburg PA
CBHW060749180626
46818CB00002B/513